John Clark Murray

Memoir of David Murray, late Provost of Paisley

With sketches of local history in his time

John Clark Murray

Memoir of David Murray, late Provost of Paisley
With sketches of local history in his time

ISBN/EAN: 9783337281779

Printed in Europe, USA, Canada, Australia, Japan

Cover: Foto ©Raphael Reischuk / pixelio.de

More available books at **www.hansebooks.com**

MEMOIR

OF

DAVID MURRAY,

LATE PROVOST OF PAISLEY,

WITH

Sketches of Local History in his Time.

BY HIS SON,

J. CLARK MURRAY, LL.D.,

PROFESSOR OF MENTAL AND MORAL PHILOSOPHY,
M'GILL COLLEGE, MONTREAL.

PAISLEY: ALEXANDER GARDNER.

1881.

PREFACE.

A SHORT time before his last illness, partly at the suggestion of friends, partly (perhaps) for amusement, Provost Murray had begun to collect materials for some sketches of local history during his long public life. After his death, it was suggested to me that his fellow-townsmen would appreciate some record of his life, embodying such local sketches; and, with the aid of these, I expected that the labour of preparing a memoir would be comparatively light. A more careful examination, however, soon disclosed the fact that the provost had been able to carry out his project but a very little way; though, from the materials which he had jotted down, and which have been largely used in the earlier chapters of this memoir, I cannot help feeling that we have lost a valuable contribution to the history of the West of Scotland. In consequence of this loss, and of my distance from all sources of information about my father's life, it has taken longer time than I had anticipated to gather materials for the main part of the memoir. In this labour I have received assistance from several friends ; but it is with special pleasure that I acknowledge the services of the Rev. Dr. James Brown, of Paisley, who has not only contributed some valuable suggestions, but has generously borne the greater part of the work of seeing the book through the press.

J. CLARK MURRAY.

MONTREAL, 10th March, 1881.

CONTENTS.

———

LIFE OF DAVID MURRAY.

———oo⋋o⋌oo———

I.—PARENTAGE.

David Murray, the Calendrer—Alexander Smith—Wealth of
the Old Paisley Manufacturers—David Dale—Birth.

OST men, who are curious enough to inquire into their ancestry, have been mor-
tified at the difficulty of penetrating to
the sources of family history. The late
Provost Murray was no exception to this general
fate. Evidently on his father's side he had never
succeeded in getting beyond his grandfather; and
in his mother's family, traditional recollections were almost equally limited. His paternal grandfather is
the relative from whom he took his name. This
earlier David Murray was a native of Caithness-shire,
somewhere—the family story said—in the neighbourhood of John o' Groat's House; but his con-

nections there have been entirely lost sight of, though apparently some correspondence was kept up for a generation or two after his migration to the south. It may be conjectured that he was attracted so far from his northern home by those inducements, which will be noticed presently, as having contributed to the rapid increase in the population of Paisley at the time. He is now remembered only as having carried on the business of a calendrer in the building on St. Mirren's Street, now known as the Anderson Hall, which still stands opposite the Royal Bank House, but is doomed to disappear under the new street-improvements.

David Murray, the calendrer, lived to the good old age of eighty-four, and during his life-time was twice married. His first wife, who was called Angus and was a native of Kinross, left a son and a daughter. The latter married a Mr. Wilson; while the son, who was named William, became the father of the late provost. It may be interesting to add that old David Murray, by his second marriage, had three daughters, one of whom deserves to be remembered for the sake of her son. The second daughter, Christina, who is the last survivor of this old family, married a Mr. Smith, and became the mother of Alexander Smith, the poet and essayist. Alexander Smith is too well known, and his life has been too often written, to require any further sketch here. It may be mentioned merely that, though born in Kilmarnock, he spent his boyhood in Paisley, to which his father's, as well as his mother's, family belonged. The novel of "Alfred Hagart's Household" draws its materials largely from old Paisley society, and it was not difficult for a man with the advantages of the late provost to recognise the originals who had suggested some of its characters. Shortly after the appearance of "A Life Drama," I remember Smith writing for the album of my eldest sister some verses, which show that he still lingered with pleasure over the reminiscences of his early home. The owner of the album and the writer of the verses have both passed into the eternal silence, and it may therefore be allowed to make the verses known to his friends, even though they do not by any means exhibit his finest lyrical touch—

> Cold the death dews on my brow,
> Bright and cold as polar morn,
> Cold is death. O colder now
> On my heart thy scorn
> Lies like snow.
>
> Round thy words and looks and smiles
> Memory lingereth, as heaves

> The ocean with most loving wiles
> On calm summer eves
> Round incense isles.
>
> When the sun is in the west,
> The ardent-hearted marigold
> Shuts his eyes.   Across my breast
> My arms I fold,
> And sink to rest.

Before leaving the poet, it may be added that his younger brother, David Murray Smith, who died under peculiarly saddening circumstances, in the spring of 1879, has also rendered some useful services in English literature.

In the year 1792, old David Murray sent his only son, William, to learn the business of a painter, and the indenture of the lad's apprenticeship is a curiosity in the local history of trade.   It seems that, in those days, an apprentice could be obtained on condition that "the master shall keep and maintain and entertain his said apprentice, bed, board, and washing, in the family with himself during the whole space of the indenture, but the apprentice to find clothing during the indenture."   Some time after completing his apprenticeship, William Murray started business with a partner ; but ultimately settled by himself in Gilmour Street, where the business he established is still carried on.

But the late Provost seemed to dwell most fondly on recollections of his mother's family, and especially of his mother's father, James Wilson. Mr. Wilson was son of a farmer in the parish of Dreghorn, Ayrshire. He had been attracted to Paisley about the year 1760, by the inducements which its successful manufactures held out to men of enterprise. It is evident that, in the latter part of last century, the manufacturers of Paisley were developing an extent of trade, which, although trivial in comparison with the vast enterprises of our own day, was yet a startling advance on the primitive production of an earlier time. The wealth thus accumulated naturally excited astonishment, if not envy, among a people accustomed to the severe poverty of old Scottish life. An interesting evidence of this may be noticed by the way in a letter of Burns. On his way home from Edinburgh in 1788, the poet passed through Paisley, where he visited his "worthy, wise friend," Mr. Pattison ; and in writing an account of the visit to his *Clarinda*, he says, "I was there ten hours : during which time I was introduced to nine men worth six thousands ; five men worth ten thousands ; his (Mr. Pattison's) brother, richly worth twenty thousands ; and a young weaver, who will have thirty thousands good when his father, who has no more children than the

said weaver and a Whig Kirk, dies."* It is no wonder that, with visions of such wealth before their fancy,
young men should have been tempted to the looms of
Paisley, from the farms and villages of Ayrshire, or even
from John o' Groat's House. James Wilson was one
of these adventurers. He came to Paisley in search of
fortune, but he went back to his native district for a
wife; and the wife, whom he brought to Paisley, is
worthy of some notice. She was called Janet Dale, or
Deall, as the name was originally spelt. Her father,
Hugh Dale, was a brother of William Dale, the father
of that David Dale, whose life is by no means forgotten
among Scotsmen yet. David Dale was born in 1739,
at Stewarton, where his father was a general store-
keeper, and in the neighbourhood of which the Dales
had been farmers for several generations before.
Though employed in boyhood at farm-work, David
Dale had been attracted at an early age, by the brilliant
prospects opened up in the rising trade of Paisley; and
it was there that he first learnt the manufacture, with

---

* Chambers' "Life and Works of Robert Burns," Vol. ii., pp.
230-1.

the extension of which in the West of Scotland his name has become associated. *

It was thus a cousin of David Dale, who married James Wilson, and became the maternal grandmother of the late Provost Murray. The old couple, about whose influence over their grandson more will have to be said by and by, lived in their later days at 22 Smithhills Street; and it was in the adjoining house, number 24, that he was born, 12th October, 1807.

---

* There is, in Chambers' " Biographical Dictionary of Scotsmen," an interesting article on David Dale, writen by " a gentleman of kindred spirit, the late Andrew Liddell, Esq., of Glasgow." (See Strang's " Glasgow and its Clubs," p. 302, note, 3rd ed.) The portrait of Dale in Kay's " Edinburgh Portraits," is said by Dr. Strang to be " a good effigy."

II.—PAISLEY AT THE BEGINNING OF THE CENTURY.

Increase in the Population of Paisley—Aspect of its Streets—
Modes of Travel—Stage-coach *versus* Canal—Journey to the
Seaside—Transmission of News—Postal Restrictions—Old
Mode of Transacting Business.

N estimating the influences amid which the boyhood of the late Provost Murray was spent, we must carry ourselves in imagination back to the state of Paisley in the second decade of the present century. Fortunately, he has himself collected a considerable quantity of material for sketching a picture of that period in a lecture which he delivered to the Philosophical Society of the town, in March, 1875, on "Reminiscences of Sixty Years in the History of Paisley." From that and a few other sources, some facts of interest for our purpose may be gathered.

About the middle of last century, the population of Paisley, which had previously never exceeded four thousand, began to increase rapidly under the attractions of the silk, linen, and gauze manufactures, for which it has since been famed. During the latter part of the century, it had risen from the modest proportions of a village to a town of 24,000 inhabitants. During the first ten years of the present century, it had added four or five thousand more, and, in 1821, the population exceeded 38,000.* It is evident, therefore, that, though in a later part of Provost Murray's life, the population of Paisley remained stationary, and its trade underwent periods of stagnation, amounting, in some branches, to absolute paralysis, his early days were passed amid the stir and excitement of rapidly-extending enterprise.

In its architectural aspects the town has undergone none of those transformations which would render it difficult for a companion of Provost Murray's childhood to find his way through its principal streets still. A stroll through these streets soon shows that, with here and there an exception, the houses are all about as old at least as the century, while many bear unmistakable traces of an earlier origin ; and the glamour of a quaint antiquity, which invests these buildings, may perhaps explain the appearance of picturesqueness they present

* "Historical Description of the Abbey and Town of Paisley," by Charles Mackie, p. 119.

to some eyes.*   It may be difficult for a visitor at the
present day, who is unaffected by memories of the past
or by the passion of antiquarianism, to catch any of
those picturesque views which the town is said to give
at some points ; but there can be no doubt that many
of the circumstances which interfere most seriously
with its amenities now,—especially the pollution of its
atmosphere and its river,—are the result of causes
which have come into operation within comparatively
recent times.   At the beginning of this century though
the Abbey garden had disappeared to make way for
what was then appropriately enough, but is now, with
a touch of unintentional irony, dubbed the New Town ;
and though the south-west winds brought up from the
evaporations of the Atlantic those masses of cloud
which still shut out the blue sky, at times for days; yet
the gloom of a clouded sunlight was not deepened by
the volumes of smoke which arise from the use of
steam power, and it was still possible for the house-
holder, who had a heart for tending flowers, to surround
his house with hues and odours, which vanish before

---

* "Memoir of Christopher North," by Mrs. Gordon, p. 1 ;
"Tannahill's The Soldier's Return," by J. J. Lamb, Introd.,
pp. i.-ii.

the pestilent fumes that issue from the numerous factories where chemical decompositions are carried on. In fact, the Paisley weavers of those old days, when their trade was one of the most remunerative in the country, were celebrated for their floriculture ; and my father retained pleasant recollections of their trim cottages with bright little gardens attached, some of which, though spoiled of all their attractiveness, may yet be seen about the districts of Maxwelton and Ferguslie.*

The loss of its amenities by the town is thus connected with a change in its society too. The mode of life in those old times must have been marked by many peculiar restrictions, owing to the absence of those very appliances of practical science which have destroyed to such an extent the pleasantness of modern towns. To a child of the present generation, probably none of

---

* One of these amateur gardeners was exhibiting his achievements to a bailie of the town, and descanting with tenderness on the points of beauty in his pets. The bailie, in whom, unfortunately, all aesthetic appreciations had been swamped by a coarse utilitarianism, confined his remarks to the single wish—"Weel, man, after a', I wad raither see a guid raw o' cabbages." "Sae wad a coo!" was the excusably testy reply of the disgusted enthusiast.

these restrictions of an older society would appear so striking as those which affected the means and the rate of locomotion.   As far as human life received a tinge from the facilities and habits of travelling, it is not too much to say that it has undergone a completer revolution during the life of Provost Murray than during all previous time.   The traveller of his early days could not proceed on his journey with greater speed than his prototype among any of the ancient nations who were far enough advanced in civilisation to build roads.   It may be questioned whether a Roman proconsul of two thousand years ago could not be conveyed to his province with less discomfort and delay, than the governor of a British colony could reach the seat of his government before the days of railways and steamers.   At the beginning of our century the most expensive, and therefore the most fashionable mode of travelling, outside of the private carriage or post-chaise, was by the mail-coach.   Like many others I had gathered, from a well-known paper of De Quincey's, as well as from other sources, some romantic illusions on the glory of that old style of locomotion; but I have often heard these illusions dispelled by my father's descriptions of the unromantic reality.   During the last few years, when he used to enjoy the conveniences of a Pullman car in travelling between Paisley and London, he was wont to reflect on the discomforts and fatigues he had to undergo in his earlier life, when forced to choose between the equally unpalatable alternatives of challenging the inclemencies of a British climate on the outside of a stage-coach, or being suffocated in its stifling interior; and we, who grumble at a delay of minutes in reaching the termination of a journey, who spend our ingenuity in constructing the saloons of railway coaches and steamboats to charm us into the pleasing illusion of being at home in our own dining-rooms and parlours, find it hard to plant ourselves in imagination among those who could be coaxed into travelling at all, when it was apt to be accompanied with so much physical suffering, when even a short journey might be delayed for days. For stories are still current in Paisley of manufacturers, about the beginning of the century, — bolder spirits, stimulated either by natural courage or by poverty to try the less costly mode of reaching London by the "smacks" which plied from Leith, and finding themselves detained, by contrary winds, for two or three weeks on the voyage.

Fortunately we have materials for a tolerably clear picture of the travel which was common around Paisley

in those old times. To Glasgow, after the canal was
opened, this became the main line of conveyance, for
those at least who were not satisfied with the means of
locomotion which Nature has provided for all. Indeed, it is astonishing that any but the aged and the
feeble were induced to pay for conveyance by the boats
originally used on the canal; for an ordinary pedes-
trian could easily beat them in a leisurely saunter to
Glasgow. Those lumbering old hulks took two hours
to be dragged from Paisley to Port-Eglinton; and the
passengers required another half-hour to find their way
to the business part of the city. Yet it is said that
this old style of travelling was not without its plea-
sures. People could settle down to the enjoyment of
each other's society in a manner which is out of the
question during the hurry and noise of a few minutes'
journey in a train. The *dambrod* was a favourite
resource for whiling away the tedium of the trip, while
those inclined could add to this healthful recreation a
grosser excitement from the stimulants for sale at the
bar. The more intellectual passengers are described
as occupying their time in discussing state affairs; and,
in the opinion of some, the political convictions developed by these discussions were quite as valuable

and independent as those obtained by glancing over the leaders of a morning daily.

After the Canal Company had accommodated the public in this homely way for some time, its shareholders were thrown into consternation by a daring speculator, Mr. Lyon, introducing a new style of coaches, dignified with the high-sounding title of "Sons of Commerce," which astonished old-fashioned travellers by making the distance of seven miles between Paisley and Glasgow in the brief space of an hour. But the benefits of competition soon became manifest. Inventive genius was quickened into fresh exertions. Mr. William Houstoun of Johnstone, produced a new specimen of naval architecture in the shape of light " gig boats," as they were called, which were drawn by a pair of horses at a speed equal to that of Mr. Lyon's coaches. The new boats proved the favourite mode of conveyance ; and the " Sons of Commerce " did not seriously interfere with the dividends, or rather did not increase the losses of the Canal Company.

Perhaps the difference between the means of travel at the present day and those available at the beginning of the century, could not be more strikingly indicated to a resident in the West of Scotland, than by describing a journey to the watering places on the Clyde during the earlier period. In those days these places were comparatively few. There were only the ancient villages, such as Gourock, and Largs, and Saltcoats; and these were still composed mainly of primitive huts, without even a foreshadowing of the charming villas and statelier mansions, by which their aspect has since been entirely transformed. The journey to these villages in my father's boyhood I have often heard him describe. The carrier, who plied between Paisley and the selected watering-place, had to be engaged beforehand. By means of straw covered with some sort of cloth, his cart was made available for human beings, with some diminution of the discomfort which its jolting inevitably entailed. In such a conveyance, even the best families of the town were content to jog along at the stately pace of a cart-horse's walk. By starting early in the morning, the more distant places, like Saltcoats or Ardrossan, could be reached before the late nightfall of summer; but those who were satisfied with Gourock or Largs, might arrive at their destination somewhat earlier in the day. Amid such obstacles to movement beyond one's immediate neighbourhood, the proverbial narrowness of the untravelled mind must have reached an exaggerated form. It is amusingly expressed in a local story, which, however imaginary, is at least truthful in picturing the mental condition of the times. A Paisley "body,"—a typical representative of the period, —had set out on his first journey from home, a trip to Largs ; and, on reaching the heights of Renfrewshire from which the magnificent panorama of the firth opens to the view, exclaimed :—"Eh, man ! It's a gran' warl' this, when a body sees 't a' ! "

At a time when the transmission of any message implied the locomotion of a messenger to carry it, and that at the rate which has been described, the communication of intelligence between different localities must have been conducted in a manner so utterly different from our own, that we find some difficulty in realising the mode of life among those whose intercourse was limited by such restrictions. During my father's last illness, I was able to telegraph from a remote watering-place on the Gulf of St. Lawrence and receive an answer from Paisley within six hours : by any of the ordinary means of transmitting messages when my father was a boy, it would usually take that time at least to communicate between Paisley and Glasgow. At present a letter may be sent for twopence halfpenny to almost every part of Europe or North America : sixty years ago a Paisley merchant paid nearly twice that sum for postage to Glasgow, and more

B

than five times as much for a London letter. The morning papers in Montreal give a summary of every important debate that is held on the previous evening, and the result of every important vote that is taken overnight, in the British Parliament : at the beginning of the century, people had to wait upon the mail-coach for news. During the great continental war, crowds were often to be seen in Paisley, wending their way along the Glasgow road, about the hour when the mail-coach was expected ; and as the distant sound of the guard's horn was heard, and the distant flash of his red coat was seen, every foot was a tiptoe, and every eye was strained to descry the appearance of the flag, which was always flaunted if the coach brought news of a victory.

These restrictions on the transmission of intelligence necessarily affected the whole style of transacting business. My father has preserved a pleasant picture of the old-fashioned trade of those days, which will form an appropriate close to this chapter. " During the closing years of last and the early years of the present century, there were a good many thread manufacturers in Paisley, though there were no steam engines nor large factories. . . . . . . These small manufacturers were on the most friendly terms with one another. There seemed to be no trade-rivalry or jealousy between them. They travelled to Glasgow every Wednesday on business by the canal. On reaching Glasgow, they found their way to an old-fashioned hostelry or carriers-quarters on the west side of High Street, one or two 'lands' from the Cross Steeple. I had once or twice the privilege of accompanying my grandfather on these Wednesday-visits; and I recollect a large apartment—half kitchen half hall—with several old tables, at one of which the old gentlemen from Paisley sat. Women from the villages and the country around Glasgow brought in their spun thread, and were paid for their past week's production. They then received a fresh supply of lint for the next week's work. The lint was got from a 'heckler,' or carder, whose shop, I presume, was contiguous. Each had his bag, into which the spun lint was packed; the bag was tied with a label-address at the neck, and left to be called for by the Paisley carrier. A plain dinner of Scotch broth, beef, and potatoes was served on the same table, at which business was transacted, there being always a dram on the table. About four or five o'clock they took the road homeward, and, except in very bad weather, walked to Paisley. When the Half-way-house was reached, they generally rested for half-an-hour, and took a refreshment of a little whiskey and water with a bit of oat-cake, which the landlady generally had ready for them.   These walks were leisurely, and must have been very enjoyable, for there was a lively conversation all the way.   I am not sure but life was as enjoyable to these men as to us.   Their houses were smaller, perhaps less comfortable, and certainly had fewer conveniences ; their businesses were not so large, nor their chances of making money so numerous ; but their wants were smaller, their tastes simpler, and they had not so much hurry and turmoil and anxiety, so much wear and tear, as the present generation in their haste to be rich."

III.—BOYHOOD AND YOUTH.

Accident on the Canal—Excitement of the War with Napoleon
—James Wilson's Household—Legendary Stories and Ballads
—Prince Charlie's Army—Mar's Year's Bairns—Old Family
Bible—Rev. James Drummond—Chap Books—Medical Ap-
prenticeship—Junior Literary Society—Letter of William
M'Oscar.

THE earliest event in his life-time that David
Murray remembered was one calculated
to leave a deep impression on his mind,
as it struck to the heart of the whole
community in which he lived. A few days after the
opening of the canal, in November, 1810, an accident
happened by which 195 passengers were precipitated
from the top of a boat into the canal-basin, and of these
85 were drowned. Although at the time he was only
one month beyond his third year, he writes in late life
that he remembered, " as if it were yesterday, the sen-
sation produced when the news began to spread
through the town. First there were groups of people
standing speaking with an awe-struck appearance;
then the streets were deserted from the people rush-

ing to the scene, to learn the fate of friends, or
merely to see the extent of the calamity; and the
carrying home of the dead bodies in the afternoon and
evening tended to deepen the impression produced."

Besides the local influences by which David Murray
was surrounded, he dwells himself upon the fact that
his boyhood was passed during the last years of the
great Continental war, which closed with the battle of
Waterloo. His boyish spirit, both in its more serious
moods and its amusements, caught a certain glow from
the military fervour which was perpetually fired by the
local, as well as by the general, incidents of the war.
"There was nothing but 'sodgerin' in those days," he
says. "Boys were accustomed to great military dis-
plays, recruiting parties, and the drilling of militia and
volunteer corps. They caught the infection, and their
favourite amusements were—to march with paper caps,
wooden swords, fifes or whistles, and all the paraphernalia of a mock military pomp." In his later days,
the provost sometimes took great delight in describing
these amusements of his boyhood, and the events of
the great war by which the amusements were suggested.

But to discover the most valuable, and perhaps also
the most powerful, of the influences by which the early

life of David Murray was educated, we must retire to the home of his maternal grandfather, James Wilson. The grandson was still in his boyhood when the grandfather died; but the memory of the old man was cherished with a charming freshness and an unfading respect when the grandson had become an old man himself. The picture, which has thus been preserved, of an old Paisley household, is illuminated with that simple nobleness which, it is to be hoped, has not yet altogether vanished from Scottish homes; and for those who find a poetic charm in human life—not only amid the serenity of rural scenes, but amid the turmoil and smoke of dingy streets—this picture may be touched with a sort of idyllic beauty.

There were many attractions about this old household. My father was the first, and for some years the only, grandchild of the old couple; and with all their Stoical virtues, it is evident that they were often tempted into the proverbial indulgence of grandparents. But it was fortunate that their society had other attractions for the grandson as well. Their memory was stored with the traditional history, the legends and ballads of Scotland; and one can almost envy my father the privilege of having learnt the legendary lore of our country from people who had been brought up in a simple rural society, where the fairy world still held a real sway over the imagination. Many a long winter evening he whiled away under the spell of the weird stories told by his grandfather, or of the romantic ballads which his grandmother could chant; and he used to trace a relic of the deep impression which these evenings had left, in a dash of superstitious fear which crept over his feelings at times even in later life. Among the historical narratives, which he was accustomed to hear at his grandfather's fireside, there is one personal reminiscence of the old man's that is not unworthy of being preserved. "My grandfather has often related to me that he saw the rebel army in 1745. He was then only about six years of age; but he described the march of the troops as seen by him from a rising ground on his father's farm. It was a bright clear morning,* and the beams of the morning sun were gleaming on the steel arms of the

---

* This must have been the 24th of Dec., 1745. On that day the Highlanders left Drumlanrig, the seat of the Duke of Queensberry, and marched through the Pass of Dalveen to Douglas Castle, (Chambers' "History of the Rebellion of 1745-6," p. 207.) Some point in Ayrshire, possibly not far from his father's farm, may have afforded James Wilson a glimpse of the Highlanders passing along the west of Lanarkshire.

rebels. My grandfather also graphically described the alarm into which the country people were thrown from fear of the exactions of the Highlanders. . . . Dreading that their pewter dishes might be appropriated for making bullets, they carefully concealed them in the *grupe*.* Here then, am I living in 1878, who have conversed with an eye-witness to an historical event at the distance of more than 130 years."†

But happily there were also other circumstances about the life of James Wilson's household which tended to leave more valuable impressions on the life of his grandson. From all the facts which have been preserved illustrative of the old man's character, it is evident that he represented a peculiarly fine type of old Scottish piety. We may assume, as a matter of course, that he exhibited at times all the sternness of

---

* "*Grupe, Groop.* A hollow behind the stalls of horses or cattle, for receiving, &c." (Jamieson's "Scottish Dictionary.")

† Another connection with a remote historical past has been preserved by Provost Murray :—" I have heard my grandmother say that her father and mother were *Mar's year's bairns.*" It may not be useless to explain that the first attempt to restore the Stuarts was made in 1715 under the Earl of Mar, and in consequence that year came to be familiarly known by the Earl's name ; so that a *Mar's year's bairn* was a child born in 1715.

character which is usually supposed to be a peculiar result of a Calvinistic education, but which must surely make its appearance under any system of education which cultivates uncompromising convictions of duty. But it is a mistake to suppose that such sternness is incompatible with a sincere delight in the harmless sports of fancy, or that it will not allow the heart to bubble over with laughter at the funnier aspects of life. At all events, it is evident that old James Wilson had not allowed the severer views of life to close up the springs of more genial feeling which God has opened in the human soul. That man must have been singularly free from the morbid egotism of the morose fanatic, who in his old age could not only retain in his memory, but retail to his grandchild, the legendary lore which he had learnt in his own childhood, and could encourage his wife to find pleasure in chanting the grand old ballads of his native land. This is all the more creditable to the old man from the fact that he was a dissenter; and it is notorious that dissent had not only absorbed a large proportion of the piety of the time, but gave special encouragement to that Puritanism which frowns on every aspect of life that is not distinctively religious, or at least moral. But the fact is, that a fair and kindly research into the religious life of old Scottish society can scarcely fail to impart a more cheerful tint to the monotonous colouring of gloom in which it has so often been depicted. James Wilson was merely one of the many in whom a healthy Christian culture left no soil for the noxious outgrowths of an ascetic and sectarian temper.

It was not to any single utterance of his grandfather that David Murray traced the valuable influence of the old man ; he speaks of it rather as due to the general impression of his life and character. But there is one feature of the grandfather's life, on which the grandson's memory dwelt with a fondness that was touching. This was his habit of family worship ; and the scene, which this habit recalls, preserves an interesting picture of a bygone time. "The old family Bible," Provost Murray writes, "which I use at family worship, has many associations for me ; and I never feel so much at home as when using it. My first recollection and impressions of family worship were received from my grandfather ; and the very oil-stains of the sacred volume are still dear to me, as bringing back with freshness those early days when I used to be present in that old fashioned kitchen in Smithhills, with its great wide fire-place, and the two old people seated on each side of it, with the glimmering light of an oil

lamp, or *crusie*, suspended from the rude chimney-
piece.   Partly from failing sight, and partly from im-
perfect light, the old man was obliged to draw so near
the lamp, that not unfrequently drops of oil fell on his
Bible ; and hence those stains that are still so visible."*

---

* A note may be welcome about this old Bible.   It bears on
its title :—" The Holy Bible, containing the Old Testament and
the New : with arguments prefixed to the different Books, and
Moral and Theological Observations at the end of every Chapter : composed by the Rev. Mr. Ostervald, Professor of Divinity,
and one of the Ministers of the Church at Neufchatle in Switzer-
land.   Translated at the desire of, and recommended by, the
Society for propagating Christian Knowledge.   Glasgow, printed
and sold by Joseph Galbraith, MDCCLXXI."   The title page gives
evidence of wear and tear, and has been pasted for preservation
on to a sheet of newer paper.   The volume has also got a new
binding in full calf,—a fine specimen of the substantial work
which many will remember as proceeding from the shop of the
Condies.   An examination of the book shows, in contrast with
common outside impressions of Scottish Calvinism, that the New
Testament in general has been more diligently read than the Old.
The large marginal oil-stains are confined to the New, extending
from about Matthew xv., to Hebrew xi., deepest towards John
and Acts, though the whole of the New Testament bears traces
of good use with occasional drops of oil.   Revelation seems to
have been least read.   In the Old Testament the oil-stains are
fewer and slighter, and the pages generally cleaner.   The only
part, whose usage comes near to that of the New Testament, is
the Psalter, Proverbs, and Ecclesiastes.   Among the historical
books, Genesis and the earlier chapters of Exodus are most

With such influences playing around him in the years of his boyhood, it is a matter of secondary importance what education David Murray received by attendance at schools. Any impress, left on him by such education, was evidently very slight in comparison with the stimulus he received from other sources. The only teacher, whose influence he could remember, was Mr. James Drummond, whom many may still recollect as minister, first of the parish, afterwards of the Free Church, of Millport.* Mr. Drummond took a personal interest in his pupil, and awakened in him the taste for a better class of literature. Previously to this period, the pupil's reading had been confined to the chap-

---

soiled, as if the owner of the Bible had been more powerfully attracted by the perennial charm of the pictures of patriarchal life with which the story of Israel opens, and had been rather repelled by the savage revolutions and cruel wars of later times.

* Mr. Drummond is not the minister of this parish, who used to pray for "The Cumbraes, larger and smaller, and the adjacent islands of Great Britain and Ireland." But it is told of him that, in his later days, when eye-sight and memory began to fail, he sometimes protracted his sermons to such a length, that, in the early dusk of a winter afternoon, his congregation, one by one, slipped away home unobserved, and the beadle had to interrupt the fervour of "the old man eloquent," by informing him that he was preaching to empty pews.

books, which seem to have been in pretty extensive
demand at the time. A collection of these works was
issued recently from the Glasgow press, and I find it
among the curiosities of my father's library. On
glancing through the collection, surprise is excited at
the undiscriminating range of the authors in the selec-
tion of subjects; for their pens seem to pass with ease
from the story of "Simple John, and his Twelve Mis-
fortunes," to the "History of the Life and Sufferings
of the Rev. John Welsh, sometime Minister of the
Gospel at Ayr," or to the "History of Mahomet, the
great Imposter, containing his Birth and Parentage, his
Wives, &c." The books are generally illustrated by
old-fashioned woodcuts; and an idea of the artistic
execution displayed may be gathered from the fact,
that the same print of a puritanical-looking parson, with
gown and bands, serves to represent the Rev. John
Welsh and Mahomet the Imposter. From such in-
sipid monstrosities of literature, David Murray was attracted by Mr. Drummond putting into his hands
"The Vicar of Wakefield," and some of the early
novels by the then unknown author of "Waverley,"
which were exciting the world's wonder and curiosity
at the time. With the reading of these and kindred
books, a new sense seemed to be awakened in the boy's

mind, and a world of undreamt glories opened to his view. Childhood, with its dependence on the intellectual influences of others, had closed ; youth was opening up with its aspirations and endeavours after self-culture.

Possibly it was the tastes engendered by Mr. Drummond, that led to his pupil selecting one of the learned professions as his occupation in life. At all events, on the first of July, 1819, he was apprenticed to Dr. Robert M'Kechnie. He completed the four years of his apprenticeship, and should then have proceeded to the University, to take the ordinary medical curriculum ; but his professional studies were never carried so far. It is understood that he acquired a dislike for the practice of surgery, which in those days it would have been impossible to separate from the practice of medicine ; and this dislike seems to have formed an influential motive in inducing him to change his plan of life. Still, he never lost the benefit of the scientific tastes and scientific culture, which he acquired, even in those early years, under Dr. M'Kechnie. The old doctor himself always regretted that his apprentice had abandoned the profession, as he had been led to form high expectations of the boy's success, from the zeal he displayed in his preliminary studies. Years afterwards, when the former apprentice began to exhibit his abilities in public life, the doctor used to say :—" If the Provost had only stuck to the profession, he wouldn't have spent his days in Paisley. He would have been among the highest in the profession at one of the universities."

During his apprenticeship, the science in which David Murray took a special interest was chemistry; and he bore to his grave a slight scar from a wound he received in the face by an explosion which occurred during the incautious performance of an experiment. His busy life, of course, prevented him from keeping pace with the rapid march of his favourite science; but to the last he continued to take a keen interest in its practical applications, especially to the manufactures of his native town. It is probably also to the studies of those distant years that we must trace the intelligence and the care which he devoted to all questions of sanitary reform.

A pleasing sketch of the general character of the young medical apprentice has been given by Dr. William M'Kechnie, to whom I am also indebted for most of my information about this period in the life of his old friend. "He was a great favourite in our house," says the doctor, "of most obliging disposition,

and always ready to lend his aid in all our difficulties
—whether of lessons or play. He was earnest, of a
quiet orderly disposition, very studious, anxious to
acquire information, and reading all manner of books.
But what I recollect of him best was his calm and self-
possessed manner. He was not easily put out with
any difficulty, and in this respect already exhibited
very much of the character which distinguished him in
after-life."

It must have been shortly after leaving the surgery
of Dr. M'Kechnie, that David Murray fell among a set
of young men forming an association that existed for
some years under the name of the "Junior Literary
Society." Mr. David Gilmour tells me that this society
met at one time in the Pen Close, and in the same
hall which he has immortalised in his charming sketch
of the quaint religious life cultivated among the "Pen
Folk;" but apparently at a later time the society removed to the Abbey Close,—I believe, to the same
room in which the Philosophical Society of Paisley
used to hold its meetings long ago. The transactions
of a club of literary youngsters in a provincial town
more than half a century ago can scarcely be of much
interest to the present generation. In many respects
this society resembled other associations which have a

similar object ; but a glance at some of its records, which still survive, shows that it succeeded in accomplishing some good work in the culture of its members. While it fell into the usual fate of such societies by squandering a good deal of time in discussing problems whose interest had long died out, if they ever had any vitality, it is pleasant to find that a large proportion of its debates were devoted to questions which expressed the real issues of intellectual and spiritual life at the time. A fact so creditable to the society implies that its meetings must have been often under the guidance of men who were in earnest about its work ; and it is interesting to find on its roll such names as those of William M'Oscar (who is remembered as an effective teacher, and could wield the pen well at times too*) and William Cross, whose romance of "The Disruption" still retains its interest with the public.

In an essay on self-culture, which David Murray delivered to the society at the opening of the year 1825, he urges on his fellow-members the obligation to take advantage of the opportunities afforded in their meetings by a previous study of the subjects to be

---

* See the "Poetical Works of William M'Oscar." London : Harrison & Sons, 1878.

discussed in the essays and debates. This precept expresses the spirit of his own example; and some idea of his work in connection with this society may be gathered from the fact, that among his papers there are five essays, with dates, which show that they were all written in the winter of 1824-5, besides a dozen other essays which have no dates attached. The means of culture afforded by association with a number of lads just emerging from their teens may not be of the highest order, but they are not to be despised; and few young men, in attendance at a university, could have devoted themselves with more thoroughness to the work of their classes; probably fewer still could have gained from their work more valuable results. It seems to have been in connection with this society that a more select association was formed for the practice of French composition or conversation; and among the early essays of David Murray there are two or three written in that language. On the whole, after an examination of the evidence, which is still to be had, of the educational work done by this society, it is not surprising that, in later life, Mr. M'Oscar should have written about it as he does in a letter to my father:—

" Upper Norwood, Surrey,
Jan. 26, 1872.

" DEAR MR. MURRAY,

When distributing the compliments of
the New Year to relatives and friends, permit me,
though somewhat tardy in doing so, to wish you and
yours the very best of them. In the landmarks of
memory, which I had recently so much heart-felt pleasure in recalling, there are few that stand out so prominently as the one close upon half a century ago
when we first met in the Abbey Close Debating
Society, the members of which, with the exception (if
I mistake not) of Mr. Hodge,* William Cross, and
yourself, have all gone to the 'unknown bourne.'

" From that time until now it would be supereroga-
tory to allude to the many ups and downs by which my
path of life has been chequered, if it were not to admit
that, but for those meetings and discussions, I would
have been utterly unable to make way to any but the
most menial or servile position. The fact of my having resided so near to Paisley afforded the opportunity
of forming acquaintance with a class of young men,
mostly my seniors, whose education and circumstances
were superior to my own, and whose talents stimulated

---

* As this volume is passing through the press, on the 11th of
December, 1880, Mr. Hodge also has passed away. Mr.
M'OSCAR himself died on the 11th of January, 1877.

me to strive to equal, if I could not surpass, them.
How far this has been verified, it would be hopeless
and foolish for me to follow. But this I will venture
to say that, at least in so far as I have been acquainted
with young men's societies in Paisley, the one to
which I have referred, and that which subsequently
sprang out of it, if indeed they were not identical,—
namely, the French Society which met weekly at Mr.
Colquhoun's,—exemplified a stability of character, and
a regard for the influence and reputation of its members, to which no other literary society can at all lay
claim. But truce to this subject, lest in enumerating
those who have variously distinguished themselves, I
may unwittingly transgress by complimenting yourself.

*   *   *   *   *   *

"Remember me kindly to the club, and all its
illustrious satellites, while I beg to remain,

Yours truly,

W. M'OSCAR."

IV.—INTRODUCTION TO PUBLIC LIFE.

Marriage—French Revolution of 1830—Death of George IV., and accession of William IV.—General Election—Declaration of the Duke of Wellington against Parliamentary Reform—Earl Grey's Reform Bill—Growth of Reform in Paisley—Sufferings of Paisley Weavers—Failure of the Canal Company—Reform Demonstration at Meikleriggs Moor, in 1820 —Secret Preparations for Rebellion—Commercial Crisis of 1825-6—The Reform Campaign in the West of Scotland—Its effects in Paisley—Rev. Dr. Burns and the King—David Murray appears as a Reformer.

HE year 1830 was an eventful one in the life of David Murray, as it was in the history of the British Empire. On the 27th of July, in that year, he married the wife who has been spared to share with him for nearly half a century the joys and sorows of wedded life. Her maiden name was Elizabeth Clark. Her father belonged to one branch of that family which, by the almost unparalleled development of a vast industry at Seedhills in Paisley, at Mile-end in Glasgow, and latterly at Newark in New Jersey, has made its name a household word in all the continents. Old John Clark, my grandfather, in his quiet business of a family grocer,

was one of those men who might be appropriately described as walking humbly with God, unambitious of any higher career than that of living soberly, righteously, and godly in the world. His wife's name was Helen Steel. There is no record of her relations; but her family came from Lesmahagow, and they preserved a tradition of being descended from John Steel of Waterhead, who made himself dangerously conspicuous on the side of the Covenanters in the reign of Charles II.

At the time when David Murray had thus formed for himself an independent home, events were occurring which were calculated powerfully to excite his interest in the public affairs, not only of Britain, but of Europe. On the very day of his marriage the Revolution took place in Paris, which resulted in the fall of Charles X. He was deeply excited over the event at the time, and long afterwards he used to speak of this coincidence. But this was not the only stirring event of that summer. About a month before, on the 26th of June, George IV. had died. The new king had, as the Duke of Clarence, been recognised as favourable to Liberalism; and when, in accordance with constitutional usage, he dissolved Parliament about a month after his accession, popular feeling was inflamed by an almost feverish curiosity about the new legislative body. The elections resulted in a house decidedly favourable to the Liberal party of the day. The practice had not then been introduced, which has been recently adopted by our statesmen, of accepting the verdict of the electors at the polls before it is formally delivered by their representatives in the House of Commons; but it was evident that the Conservative Government of the day, which had the Duke of Wellington at its head, could not long avoid a vote implying want of confidence. This prospect was rendered inevitable, even on the first day of the session, during the debate on the Address, by the famous declaration of the Duke against Earl Grey's suggestion to quiet the excitement following upon the French Revolution by granting a measure of Parliamentary reform.* Notwithstanding the explanations of this celebrated utterance, which appear in the recently published volume (the eighth) of the Duke's " Despatches and Correspondence," it is not surprising that his words were accepted as a declaration of war against all attempts at reform in the system

* See " Annual Register," for 1830, p. 155. The declaration is quoted at length in Alison's " History of Europe from 1815 to 1852," Chapter xxii. 73.

of Parliamentary representation. The famous statement was made on the 2nd of November; on the 15th the Government found themselves in a minority of twenty-five. It was on a comparatively unimportant point that the Government were defeated; but it is well known that they chose to go out on this point in order to avoid committing themselves on the vaster question of Parliamentary reform, which stood for discussion on the following day. The Administration of Earl Grey, which succeeded that of Wellington, introduced the Reform Bill which was ultimately carried through both houses of Parliament about two years afterwards. The history of the great movement, which resulted in the remodelling of the British legislature, belongs to the general history of the empire; but it will not be inappropriate to trace, amid the general storm, the particular wave that broke on the community of Paisley, and roused the untried energies of its late Provost.

The community of Paisley had been peculiarly prepared for being stirred by the excitement of the time. Towns have in all ages formed the centres, in which new ideas originate, and from which they emanate to revolutionise the country at large. Paisley was a town of intelligent artisans; and it has been often observed that

those engaged in manufactures are less inclined to pas-
sive obedience, less submissive to political inequalities,
than an agricultural population.   The liberalism of
Paisley, however, was apparently of late and slow growth.
As long as the inhabitants found remunerative employment in the various branches of spinning and weaving,
which added so rapidly to the wealth and population
of the town, there was no show of discontent with the
existing condition of things.   There had, indeed, been
a reform meeting held on the High Churchhill, so far
back as in 1792 ; but the movement was far from
being popular for some time.   The shock of the French
Revolution scared all moderate men, and terrified dis-
appointed Radicals into an irrational Toryism.   Reformers continued long to be stigmatised by the nick-
name of *blacknebs ;* and when Fox paid a visit to
Paisley, it is said there were only three persons in the
town of the same political stripe with himself, who were
in a social position to entertain him.   But the return
of peace in 1815, after nearly a quarter of a century
spent in war, produced a violent disturbance in the
commercial relations of men, while the rapid extension of steam-power to manufacturing processes left
without employment a large quantity of the skilled
labour which had enjoyed excellent remuneration be-

fore. The discontent of men in such circumstances is always likely to take a political turn, even though their sufferings may not have the remotest connection with their political condition ; but when we consider some of the facts of the time, we are not astonished that the manufacturing classes generally throughout the country, should have concluded that political causes were in some measure to blame for the prevailing distress. If there had been no other grievance, the corn-laws alone made it evident that the legislators of the time were not unwilling to make the bread of the poor man dear, in order to enrich the wealthy proprietor of land. The effect of these laws, in years when the British harvest was scanty, must have been appalling, especially among the working class ; for the natural and artificial scarcity combined sometimes made it impossible to obtain bread at any price. "It is told of Paisley, during a time of scarcity, that the town was often utterly without grain or meal, and that, when a dealer was fortunate enough to secure a small supply, the hungry people crowded in eager competition to his shop."*

---

* "The Nineteenth Century: a History." By Robert Mackenzie. Book ii. Chap. i.

In the histories of the period, the sufferings of the artisans of Paisley are often taken as illustrative of the distress generally prevalent throughout the country. This was undoubtedly in a large measure owing to the fact, that spinning and weaving, which formed the principal industries of the town, and which had been so comfortably remunerative for generations before, were precisely those manufactures in which the amount of labour required had been most rapidly diminished by inventions, like those of Arkwright and Cartwright, as well as by the use of steam-power. Well might Carlyle write as he does in a beautiful letter to Chalmers :—" Alas ! the poor of this country seem to me, in these years, to be fast becoming the miserablest of all sorts of men. Black slaves in South Carolina, I do believe, deserve pity enough ; but the black is at least not stranded, cast ashore, from the stream of human interests, and left to perish there : he is connected with human interests, *belongs* to those above him, if only as a slave. Blacks, too, I suppose, are cased in a beneficent wrappage of stupidity and insensibility : one pallid Paisley weaver, with the sight of his famishing children round him, with the memory of his decent independent father before him, has probably more wretchedness in his single heart, than a hundred blacks." *

The distress of Paisley, however, was enhanced by the loss of a considerable amount of local capital in an unfortunate project. The canal, which passes through Paisley from Glasgow to Johnstone, was originally intended to connect the great city of the West with the port of Ardrossan.† The company's charter contemplated a capital of £140,000, with borrowing powers to the extent of £30,000. But the capital subscribed was never more than £46,000. To carry on the work the additional £30,000 were borrowed; and the leading shareholders advanced a sum of £13,000, then a further sum of £12,000. After all, however, the work had to be left incomplete; it remained an unproductive investment, and many of the shareholders were ruined. It was in these circumstances that, in 1816, the magis-

---

* Hanna's "Memoirs of Dr. Chalmers," vol. iv. p. 200.

† The Earl of Eglinton was one of the chief promoters of the canal, and the port at its Glasgow end received its name from him. The fine harbour of Ardrossan remains as one of the most substantial results of the scheme. It may be added that, while I am writing, a bill is being promoted to convert the canal into a railway.

trates of Paisley addressed a memorial to the Lords of
the Treasury, calling attention to the extraordinary
distress which the town was suffering from the unpre-
cedented depression of its trade.   The memorial expressed the inability of the magistrates to meet the
wants of the impoverished community by means of
private subscriptions, and begged accordingly assistance
from the Government, suggesting especially that those
who had been thrown idle might be employed in the
completion of the Glasgow, Paisley, and Ardrossan
Canal.

It is needless to say that the Government did not
accede to the petition of the memorialists.   The consequence was that the distress in Paisley deepened, as
it did in other manufacturing districts as well.   With
the distress the political discontent also became intensified, till it culminated in the political troubles of 1819-
20.   The artizans of Paisley took no insignificant part
in the meetings and processions and other demonstra-
tions, by which the people paraded their political
grievances and political claims at the time.   There
was one demonstration especially which, though it did
not result in the unhappy bloodshed of the famous
meeting at Manchester about a month before, yet

attracted a good deal of attention.* On the 11th September, 1819, a large body of reformers formed a procession to Meiklcriggs moor, where a meeting was held, at which the oratory usual on such occasions was freely indulged in. The meeting, as soon as advertised, had been prohibited by a proclamation of the sheriff and magistrates, and was, therefore, in so far, illegal. Its proceedings, however, were not interrupted till the return of the procession, when the flags were seized by order of the magistrates. The enthusiastic crowd were naturally excited by this action; a riot arose, during which a considerable amount of property was destroyed or plundered; for some days disturbances were renewed, and it was only after a troop of cavalry had been called in from Glasgow, that quiet was restored. The scenes of those days had evidently left a deep impression on the young mind of David Murray.

All during the following winter the country was evidently in a very disquieted state, and secret preparations on an extensive scale were being made for open rebellion. In the spring of 1820 the peace of a Sunday morning, the 2nd of April, was disturbed by a

---

* A full account is given in the "Annual Register" for 1819, pp. 109-110.

proclamation of a most alarming character posted all
over the walls in Paisley, as well as in Glasgow and the
neighbouring towns. The proclamation professed to
issue from a committee formed to organise a provisional
government ; and, among other announcements, *com-
manded* all persons to desist from work from that day
forward. The anxiety, excited by this manifesto, was
intensified by its effects on the following day. In
Paisley, as elsewhere, manufactures were generally
abandoned ; and wherever any operatives made their
appearance for carrying on their labours, they were
obliged to quit by a secret, but effective intimidation.*
Fortunately the crisis passed without the serious con-
sequences that had been feared ; but the distress
among the weavers of Paisley continued to demand
anxious consideration. The attention of the House of
Commons was called to the subject by a petition from the
mechanics of Paisley, praying that the Government
would afford them the means of emigration to one of
the colonies. The petition was presented by Mr.
Maxwell, the member for Renfrewshire,—Paisley had
then no member ; and in his speech on the occasion,

---

* "Annual Register," for 1820, pp. 37-39.

Mr. Maxwell made some startling revelations with regard to the destitution, of which the petition was an evidence. The petition was presented on the 1st of June ; on the 29th, Mr. Maxwell returned to the subject by moving for a Select Committee to inquire into the distress of the cotton-weavers, and the possibility of devising means for their relief. The motion led to a lengthy and interesting debate, but was afterwards withdrawn.*

Between the troubles of 1819-20, and the commencement of the regular campaign for parliamentary reform, Paisley, along with other parts of the country, had to pass through another crisis of commercial failure with its attendant distress. The summer of 1826 was marked by a drought almost unexampled in the moist climate of Great Britain, and the harvest accordingly was far below the wants of the population.† The corn-laws and other restrictions of a barbarous tariff excluded the surplus food of foreign countries, and re-

---

* "Annual Register," for 1820, pp. 78-81.

† Ibid., for 1826, pp. 173-4. This was the disastrous year made memorable in the literary history of Scotland by the failures of John and James Ballantyne, and of Constable & Co., in which Sir Walter Scott was ruined.

D

duced the people in many places to actual starvation.
The suffering and consequent discontent became so
alarming, that the Government issued a " Letter from
the King to the Archbishops of Canterbury and York
for a collection in aid of the subscriptions entered into
for the relief of manufacturing classes in the United
Kingdom."* By this means a considerable sum was
raised to relieve the destitution prevailing in different
localities Paisley obtained a share of this charitable
fund ; and the relief of the starving people was entrusted to a committee, who found work for the unemployed on the river and at the "moss" in the
neighbourhood.

These events will help to explain the intensity of
feeling with which the people of Paisley threw themselves, in 1830-32, into the agitation for Parliamentary
reform. The circumstances under which the question
was introduced into Parliament as a Government
measure have been already related. We know, from
a leading member of the Administration, that it was
their policy to give the popular excitement time to
grow throughout the country, in order that the pressure

---

* "Annual Register," for 1826, p. 189, (Chronicle.)

of public opinion might exert its full effect on the legislature* ; and certainly their policy evinced by its results
a great deal of practical tact in the management of
popular feeling.   The universality and violence of the
agitation throughout the country took probably all
parties by surprise.   The West of Scotland was behind
no other section of the Kingdom in its eagerness to
secure the desired political boon.   Mass meetings were
held all over the district, at one of which in Glasgow
the numbers were estimated at 120,000 ; and we have
a vivid impression of the depth to which the excitement
penetrated society, as well as of the change in the mode
of transmitting intelligence, when we picture Sir Daniel
Sandford charmed out of his academic repose, and
frequently galloping some miles beyond the city to be
merely an hour or two earlier in obtaining news of the
latest stage in the progress of the Reform Bill.†   We
have also an evidence of the excitement in Paisley, and
of its apparent effect even on the trade of the town, in
the account of an interview with the King, which the
Rev. Dr. Burns enjoyed in 1832, shortly before the

---

* "Life and Times of Lord Brougham," written by himself,
Vol. III., p. 105.

† Strang's "Glasgow and its Clubs," pp. 447-8.

passage of the Reform Bill.   The King had,—perhaps
a relic of his sailor-frankness,—what Brougham calls
"a bad habit "* of talking too freely with all sorts of
people on public questions ; and it is not surprising
that Dr. Burns should have found His Majesty " free
and easy in his conversation, which turned principally
on two topics, very diverse from each other—the history of his ancestors of the persecuting house of
Stuart, and the reception of the Reform Bill among
the then starving weavers of the 'gude town' of Paisley."   In the course of this conversation, the King was
led to ask whether any cause could be assigned for the
depression of trade in the town.   Dr. Burns replied
that it was "generally ascribed to the great agitation
caused by the Reform Bill, and we do not look for any
improvement until it is passed."†

Of course the reply of Dr. Burns reflects merely the
impressions of the Reform party, of which he was one
of the earliest supporters among the parochial clergy ;
but such impressions enable us to understand why men

---

* "Life and Times of Lord Brougham," written by himself,
Vol. III., pp. 94-5.
† "Life and Times of the Rev. Dr. Burns," edited by his son,
pp. 96, and 110-13.

carried on the campaign against the incongruities in the system of Parliamentary representation with feelings resembling those of religious crusaders. Into this crusade, it is not surprising that David Murray threw himself with the enthusiasm of a young reformer, the brilliance of whose ideals had yet to be dimmed by the shadows of a sobering experience. Young as he was, his mind had been occupied for years with the important questions of political and social reform, which came up for settlement in Britain after the problems of the great Continental war had been solved, for a time at least, by the close of Napoleon's career at Waterloo. The essays which he wrote for the Junior Literary Society discuss, among other questions of the day, Catholic Emancipation, the right of settling private quarrels by duel, the reforms in criminal law which were demanded by Sir Samuel Romilly and Sir James Mackintosh. The subject of Parliamentary Reform itself is treated in one of those juvenile papers, which must have been written before 1828, when the Junior Literary Society became defunct. David Murray had thus prepared himself for expounding and defending the principles of Parliamentary Reform long before it was made the subject of a Government measure. It was at the public meetings held in Paisley, to promote

the Reform Bill, that he made his first appearance as
a speaker beyond the hall of the Literary Society ; and
seemingly the impression produced by these appearances stamped him at once as a rising public man.   It
was a result of the prominence thus obtained that he
was brought forward as a candidate for municipal
honours, or rather for municipal labours, in 1836.   It
is not surprising, when his age is considered—he was
under thirty—that he was elected on that occasion by
a majority of only two votes.   His election, however,
introduces us to his first period of public service.

V.—FIRST PERIOD OF PUBLIC SERVICE.

The Old Town Councils—Provost Murray's First Election to the
Council—Distress of 1826—Distress of 1841-3—General
Bankruptcy—Insolvency of the Burgh.

IMMEDIATELY after the people of Britain
had obtained the larger measure of Parliamentary Reform, it became impossible
to deny them the smaller measure of a
reform in their municipal system. At the time when
the Reform Bill was passed in 1832, the Town Councils
of Scotland were self-elected; in other words, the
provost and magistrates could either re-elect themselves at the expiry of each term, or, if any became tired
of official cares, they elected their successors. It was
essential to a body founded on such a system that
they should preserve an imposing dignity in the eyes
of those whom they took upon themselves to represent, and that may be a reason why they continued
the picturesque usages of an antique age, which seems
very far away from the prosaic life of our time. In

those days, the magistrates of Paisley still recognised
with pompous show the national establishment of
religion.   They met each Sunday morning in the old
Council Chambers, bedizened not only with the gold
chain which is still worn as a symbol of office, but with
the courtly costume of knee-breeches, silk stockings,
and cocked hat; and then, preceded by four town-
officers in scarlet coats and with glittering halberts,
they marched in stately solemnity to the High Church.
During the long reign of George III., as often as his
birthday—the fourth of June—came round, as the
loyalty of the time was apt to be somewhat jovial, it
was the custom of the magistrates to appear on the
head of the stairs in front of the old Municipal Buildings at the Cross, and there, in sight of an envious
multitude, drink a bumper to the old King's health.
The empty glasses were then tossed into the air, in
order that, having been honoured by such a ceremony,
they might never be degraded to any baser use.

It was to such a body of dignified old gentlemen
that municipal government was entrusted long ago,
without any control from the people whose affairs they
managed.   It is not to be supposed that this unchecked
administration of public funds gave rise to all the
abuses for which it certainly gave opportunity, or that

such abuses are avoided by giving the people the right of electing their municipal representatives. It is acknowledged that the affairs of Paisley were, on the whole, fairly and wisely managed by the old Town Councils; and certainly no municipal corporation of those unreformed times, even among the most corrupt of the English pocket burghs, was ever charged with the appalling scoundrelism, by which in recent years the city government of New York has been disgraced. Still, under the old municipal system, there were, especially in England, some very gross misapplications of public money, against which the people possessed no remedy; while, under the representative system, if such abuses occur, the people have only to blame their own want of interest in the management of their affairs. On the whole, therefore, it was well that the reform in the representative system of Great Britain was, in 1835, extended to municipal councils. It was in the following year, at the first election under the new law, that David Murray entered the Town Council of Paisley.

It is not without a reason that, at the close of last chapter, he was described as having been a candidate for municipal labours rather than for municipal honours; for during his connection with the Town Council his public duties absorbed a large share of the work of

his daily life. It is an evidence at once of his willing-
ness to work, and of the confidence reposed in him by
his fellow-councillors, that, the year after his entrance
into the Council, he was elected Treasurer; he became
Senior Bailie in 1840; and in 1844, he was raised to
the position of Chief Magistrate, to which he was re-
elected at the expiry of his term in 1847. There is
probably no period in the history of Paisley which has
entailed such severe and anxious labour on its municipal representatives as those fifteen years, during
which Provost Murray first gave his services to the
community. This was caused by the fact that the
town had to suffer in these years a commercial depression which, in duration and devastating effects, exceeded any distress experienced either before or since.
"Happily," said Provost Murray to his townsmen a
few years ago, "we do not know much now of the
difficulties of the magistrates and local authorities on
such occasions as the one referred to. There is no
more painful position to be placed in than to have a
mass of people in a state of absolute starvation and
destitution, without the means of supporting them, and
with the difficulty of improvising machinery that would
sufficiently test the character of the cases, and administer relief, so as to maintain the independence of

parties and take care in regard to imposition, and at the same time preserve the peace of the town. Magistrates have a most difficult duty to discharge when such a difficulty is forced upon them."

The distress, from which the people were suffering in 1826, had abated for about ten years; but it is evident that, even in that interval, the trade of the town was far from being in a healthy state, and that there could be no permanent improvement until its operatives should find occupation in some other industries than those in which machinery had driven manual labour out of the field. Accordingly the distress began again in 1837, and became so severe that the authorities were obliged to appeal to the Government. The provost and the Parliamentary representative of the burgh, along with the Lord-Lieutenant of the County, obtained an interview with the Chancellor of the Exchequer, Mr. Spring Rice, who was so impressed with their representations, that he made an advance of £2000 from the Treasury. The advance was made on the bond of the applicants; but it is said that, as they were retiring, Mr. Rice whispered to the provost :—" I hope you understand that you need not give yourself much uneasiness about the bond."

The distress was soon mitigated for a while, but it

broke out again with appalling symptoms in 1841, and continued, with little intermission, for two years. It began in April, 1841, though for some weeks it was not so serious as to be beyond the power of local efforts; but in July the numbers requiring relief had risen above two thousand. From that time to the middle of winter, the number of the destitute steadily increased till it touched at one time 17,000, and stood for some months at 14,000. No means at the disposal of an impoverished community, no exertions even of the most laborious sympathy, could cope satisfactorily with the magnitude of such suffering. Provost Murray, though he had by this time the entire charge of his private business thrown upon himself by the death of his father, spent weeks in London, along with the Rev. Dr. Burns and the Rev. Dr. Baird, endeavouring to press the alarming state of the town on the attention of the Government, and to obtain assistance from mer- chants in the Metropolis connected with the trade of Paisley. By contributions from these merchants, as well as from other sources, the distress was met till March, 1842, when the Government became at last alarmed, and despatched two Commissioners of the Poor Law to organise means for relieving the destitution of the town. These gentlemen were kept at work for two or three months, but the committee which they organised was not in a position to give up its labours before May, 1843. During these two years of destitution, over £53,000 in cash were expended by the relief committee, besides large contributions of meat, oat-meal, and other articles of food. For a while the expenditure was kept up to threepence a-day for each person under relief, but for a long time it was only one penny. I have heard my father say long afterwards, that many a morning during those dreary months he rose from his bed with the dreadful consciousness that he knew of no means for keeping the starving population in existence during the day. It was with trembling anxiety that he used to receive his budget of letters by every mail to see if there were among them any registered, as they were likely to contain remittances for the use of the relief committee; and when he unclosed a larger remittance than usual,—a £20 or £50 note,—he would flaunt it at the breakfast table with a touching childishness in his joy. No wonder that, on giving an account of those days in later life, he should have said that "the deep gloom which hung over the community at that time,—the wretched appearance of the people, the thousands waiting on the soup-kitchens, the squalor and misery everywhere in houses, in clothing,—have left an impression on my mind never to be effaced." " The feeling of those days," he said on another occasion, " was something like what one might be supposed to have in a place visited with a plague, when every man wished he could have fled from the town."

The commercial distress of this period culminated in a misfortune which forms the most serious crisis in the municipal history of Paisley. The idleness of such a large number of the operatives in the town implied that the capital, invested in the manufactures in which these operatives had been employed, was melting away. As the manufacturers became insolvent, the shopkeepers and other tradesmen, dependent on the manufacturers and their employés, were ruined too. A tide of general bankruptcy set in, which swept away about three quarters of a million sterling from the town. Inevitably, all property in the place became thus seriously depreciated. As a consequence, the municipal revenue decreased over £500 in one year, and it fell short of the expenditure by £263. When these facts became known, the credit of the burgh was at once affected. Unfortunately, its principal creditors were not wealthy capitalists who could afford to wait till their debtor recovered from the losses inevitable in a time of depression. The municipality had borrowed, in small sums at call, from a large number of persons who wanted merely a safe investment for their moderate savings. In consequence of the prevalent distress, many of the poor creditors stood in want of the money they had thus invested, and all became anxious about the security of their investments. A panic arose. A run was made on the town-chamberlain, and he was obliged at last to stop payment. Amid the general confusion, fortunately some heads remained cool enough to struggle for order, and order was soon restored. Application was made to Parliament for the creation of a Trust, to which the estate of the burgh was handed over for the benefit of its creditors. This Board of Burgh Trustees continued to administer the estate for some thirty years, when it was relieved of its functions by a measure which will be noticed in a subsequent chapter.

VI.—ECCLESIASTICAL AND RELIGIOUS WORK.

Retirement from the Provostship—Other Public Labours—
Ecclesiastical Connections—Position in the Disruption Con-
troversy—Pamphlet of Dr. Burns—Election as Deacon, as
Elder, as Session-Clerk—Religion in the family—Sabbath
School at Home—Work in the Eldership—Practical character
of Religion.

ITH the unusually arduous duties devolving
on him as a magistrate of Paisley during
the disastrous period sketched in last
chapter, David Murray could have found
little or no time to devote to other social labours. Few
men dependent on their own exertions for a living
could have given so much of their time and energy to
the service of others in any form. It is unnecessary
now, and to him it would have been distasteful at any
time, to dwell upon the extent to which his private
interests were sacrificed in his public labours. It is
much more pleasing and important to notice the fact,
that the long and earnest service, which he was called
to render to the people during his early manhood, seems

to have determined that character which made his subsequent life so valuable to his native town. Whether,
if he had had the opportunity, his fine business energies could ever have been thrown into a private
enterprise with the enthusiasm which he displayed in
the management of public affairs, it is useless to inquire ; but it appears as if, from this time, his tastes
were irrevocably determined, and it became essential
for him to find some scope for the administrative abilities which his experience had cultivated.

His retirement from the Provostship was, therefore,
merely the occasion of his entrance into other spheres
of public labour. We have seen that, when the
municipality became bankrupt, its property was placed
under the management of trustees for the benefit of
its creditors. Provost Murray remained a member of
the trust thus created nearly the whole period of its
existence. The first public office he ever undertook
was that of Manager of the Poor in 1832, and we have
seen that the relief of the unemployed formed a peculiarly prominent subject of anxiety to him and the
magistrates of Paisley during his connection with the
Town Council. All his life afterwards, the problems
of pauperism engaged a large share of his attention,
and he devoted a considerable amount of time to the

E

practical mitigation of its evils as a member of the
Parochial Boards of Paisley, as well as in other ways.*
The history of the Paisley Infirmary, which has become
an institution of extensive beneficence, is closely associated with Provost Murray's name, as he was connected
with its management from 1835 to the day of his death.
There is another institution also, in the origination of
which he took an active part, and over which he pre-
sided as long as he lived,—the Government School of
Design.   His own trade obliged him to take an interest
in art as applied to house decoration ; and his taste in
this direction would, in a larger field than his impoverished native town, have brought him very extensive occupation.   His knowledge of art, however, and
his interest in its applications, were by no means
limited to his own trade.   Many have expressed
admiration at the freshness and value of the suggestions
he was always ready to throw out at the periodical
meetings of the School of Design.   I find besides,

---

* Provost Murray and his pastor, Dr. Burns, had a ground on
which their sympathies met in their common interest in the problems of pauperism.   On the whole, the best discussion of the
Poor Law of Scotland in all its aspects is the well-known work
of Dr. Burns.

among other papers on artistic subjects, an elaborate lecture on the history of the different styles of art, which was read to the Philosophical Society of Paisley; and it would be a mistake to suppose that the lecture was a mere combination of materials got together for the nonce. He had evidently made himself familiar with the subject for years; and his information was ready at any moment to crop out, when opportunity required, in private conversation. The mention of the Philosophical Society suggests another institution with which Provost Murray was associated, though not so prominently, during the greater part of his life. It was partly in connection with this society that he cultivated his own literary and scientific tastes; and he always attached great value to the pursuits of such institutions in elevating men above the gross gratifications and petty vanities by which a true civilisation is impeded. It was, therefore, a very great pleasure to him to see the influence of the Philosophical Society extended, and the opportunities of intellectual culture so greatly enlarged by the erection of the magnificent Library and Museum, which the town owes to the liberality of his old friend, Sir Peter Coats.

The labour of the ex-provost in the various directions indicated can be but faintly imagined from such a brief statement as the above. It was only when I had examined his correspondence and other papers,—only when I bore in mind that even the large mass of MS. which he left to my care contained merely the documents which he had thought it worth while to preserve, —that i began to realise the amount of beneficent industry which he had accomplished in these various occupations. It is but just to his memory that this should be kept in view, when some account is given of the ecclesiastical and religious work that he overtook at the same time.

Provost Murray was baptised and brought up in the Church of Scotland. At the time, dissent was a comparatively small factor in the ecclesiastical life of the country; and its power was dissipated by numerous divisions into Secession and Relief, and Burgher and Anti-Burgher, and other minor sects, whose quarrels many of the present generation may have heard explained, but few can ever comprehend, and fewer still can remember. Though belonging to the national church, the provost lived amid influences which kept him from falling either into the Pharisaic illusion that there is any superior sanctity necessarily attached to a state-church, or into that ecclesiastical snobbery which looks down upon dissent as occupying a lower position in the social scale. His grandfather, James Wilson, who has been already described as exercising such an ennobling influence on his boyhood, was an elder in one of the Relief churches. Many of his companions also were dissenters, and his wife belonged to a family whose branches have long been conspicuous in the support of dissent throughout the West of Scotland. Apart from these influences, his political sympathies were all hostile to the existence of privileged classes, and ultimately led him, I believe, to favour Disestablishment as a demand of political justice.

I think it probable also that it was his political sympathies, to a large extent, that led him to take the side to which he attached himself in the great ecclesiastical struggle that culminated in the Disruption of 1843. During the ten years of that struggle, he was too entirely occupied with municipal affairs, and with the relief of an appalling pauperism, to devote any time to ecclesiastical questions; and therefore it is impossible to tell with certainty the special reasons by which he may have been led to play the part he took in the great church movement of those days. But there need be no difficulty in seeing here the same course of thought at work, by which he was induced to throw himself into the agitation for political reform. It would,

indeed, be a shallow view of the period, which looked
on the so-called evangelical movement in the Church
of Scotland as merely a ripple on the great wave of
reform-excitement, by which the political world had
been for some years before disturbed.   But a view
which ignored the influence of political causes in the
ecclesiastical sphere, or which did not, with more truth,
see in both spheres at this time evidence of the same
significant fact,—of a people awakening to a consciousness of their rights,—would betray an equally inade-
quate insight into the connection of events.   In the
case of Provost Murray, the interaction of political and
ecclesiastical sympathies must have been peculiarly
strong in determining his position in this conflict. He
does not seem, before the Disruption, to have taken
any very active interest in church-work, such as might
have drawn him insensibly into association with the
practical earnestness of the evangelical party.   Moreover, as he was not in the heat of the conflict, and
could therefore more coolly survey the situation, it is
not likely that he would have adopted the extremely
high-church line of argument, by which the evangelical
position was at times defended.   From subsequent
conversations with him, I do not think that he would
have allowed to any church, Established or Free, a

"spiritual independence" verging on that claimed by the champions of ultramontanism in the Roman Catholic Church.

This appears to be confirmed by the position which his pastor, the Rev. Dr. Burns, took in the controversy. That position was long the subject of local discussion. There are men who never know the pain of being obliged by practical necessities to decide between opposite lines of conduct, while realising that a good deal may be said on both sides,—men who reason themselves into the belief that only one course is right, and cannot comprehend how any man can reasonably adopt any other. To such men the conduct of Dr. Burns seemed an instance of weak vacillation, remarkable in a man of his vigorous understanding. But there are, fortunately, minds which sweep a wider range of thought than can be compassed by the machinery of a one-sided logic; and when the story of the Disruption controversy comes to be written by the disinterested historian, it will be found that on both sides there were men of finer nature, who shrank to the very last from the conclusions to which they were shut up by the remorseless argumentation of the mere partisan. Dr. Burns was evidently one of those who, even in the confusion of a conflict, can see that different lines of conduct may be followed with the best intention, and therefore hesitate about their own course till a crisis forces them to a decision.   He was not in Edinburgh when the Disruption occurred ; and when it was announced to him in Paisley, he would not believe it—declared it, with his peculiar accentuation, to be "impothible."   For some days after the decisive step had been taken by the great body of the Free Church, he remained in the Establishment, and evidently excited anxiety among his friends as to what his ultimate course might be.   His hesitancy at the crisis receives explanation from a pamphlet of his, the existence of which, in all probability, has been wholly unknown.   The pamphlet was printed, but never published, though the copy I possess is a proof containing the author's corrections with a view to publication.   It may have been that the immediate and unexpected development of events had rendered the publication useless.   But there is nothing in the work by which the memory of Dr. Burns can be injured, and it forms an interesting curiosity in the local history of a great national movement.

The pamphlet was written at the beginning of December, 1842, immediately after that meeting of the Non-Intrusionist clergy which, in the history of

the movement, is styled the Convocation. At this
meeting, or soon afterwards, some 480 ministers had
pledged themselves to resign their livings if the claims
of the Church were not granted by Parliament. It
is from this pledge that Dr. Burns dissents in his
pamphlet, which is entitled, *Reasons for Non-Resigna-
tion.* The keynote of its general tone is struck at the
opening by an attack upon a happy antithesis of Dr.
Chalmers' "in one of his brilliant speeches at the
Convocation :"—"It is not *we* that go out ; it is the
endowments that go out." Dr. Burns felt at the time
that, though "loudly cheered," the saying "involved
a grievous fallacy. The endowments *do not* go out at
all. They remain the patrimony of what will still be
the Established Church of the land—the badge and
the blessing of an institute from which, by the secession
contemplated, nine-tenths of all that is truly valuable
and praiseworthy shall be swept away. . . . . .
Dr. Chalmers says, '*we* don't go out.' I say, we do.
We are greatly mistaken if we suppose that all we surrender by going forth from our parishes is the pecuniary
endowment. We surrender a great deal more. We
surrender our high station as the accredited clergy of
a Christian Establishment. We throw aside all that
influence which attaches to the position for which our

forefathers contended so nobly, and at a much costlier
price than we." The author then proceeds to explain
his position more definitely. He objects to the pledge
taken at the Convocation inasmuch as it does not
specify "the precise measure, or kind of measure, the
refusal to grant which would be the turning-point of
our decision. *As it is*, every man who signs the pledge
appears to be left at liberty to judge of the measure
which the legislature may propose as he chooses; and
thus every one remains the keeper of his own conscience, and the pledge is null." What kind of measure
Dr. Burns would demand from Parliament he leaves
little room to doubt or misunderstand. He almost
ridicules the inadequacy of the Veto Act—the Act
which gave to congregations the right to veto the
presentation of a patron to any living; and he declares
it "absolute madness" to expect the legalisation of
such an Act by Parliament. Dr. Burns, it will be
remembered, was, like Provost Murray, an enthusiastic
political reformer; and nothing could satisfy him but
the unqualified abolition of patronage—the full and
free right of Christian congregations to choose their
own pastors. Any other spiritual independence he re-
fuses to recognise; the claim of "absolute supremacy"
for the proceedings of an ecclesiastical body he pro-

nounces inadmissible even in the case of a voluntary organisation. "So long as men keep within their own line, as laid down by mutual agreement, they are safe. But I am yet to learn that it is *impossible* for a small sect, say of Baptists or Congregationalists, for instance, to act in a way so contrary to the privileges of a British subject who chances to be in communion with them, and this under all the paraphernalia of spiritual or ghostly discipline, as to entitle the man to step out of the ordinary line and sist them before the civil courts of his country. They cannot interfere with the rules of the society ; but they can punish for non-adherence to their own rules, and for a wanton outrage on character or property under a religious mask. And is this wrong ? "

So far, therefore, from seeking for spiritual independence by separation from the State, Dr. Burns has " always understood it to be one of the *benefits* of a Church Establishment, that thereby a guarantee was furnished in favour of the privileges of the Church, and a check put on its excrescences. 'Hold there!' say my much-esteemed brethren, 'the first of these, but not the second !' I am not sure whether States have been in the way of granting the one without granting the other. Both are to my mind very wholesome. The State subjugating the Church produces Erastianism. The Church subjugating the State issues in Popery. *Our* union stands against both; but the theory of *absolute independence* leads to both. If the State is strongest, down goes the Church, and an Erastian monster rears its head. If the Church is strongest—and what has been may be—up goes Popery, and farewell to the liberties of mankind."

In "redding the marches" between the civil and the ecclesiastical spheres, practical difficulties may, of course, frequently arise; and Dr. Burns, therefore, sees clearly that there must be some ultimate authority for deciding where the boundary has, in any special instance, been overstepped. On this subject, also, he is unhesitating in his opposition to any ultramontane tendency. "See," he says, "that you have got good laws for your mutual regulation. . . . . And if the laws are good, and in keeping with the Word of God, I care not who shall be their accredited interpreter. Only, let there be *one* interpreter; and common sense would say, let that interpreter be the party to whom the national will has committed the right, the trust, and the power of making them effectual."

" After all," concludes the Doctor, it is not likely that I will be found like Derwent Conway's 'last man,' amid the ruins of the devoted city. I anticipate no such crisis; and I think too well of my brethren in the ministry, to leave them unwarned in a position so perilous as that which they have assumed. Let them denounce the laws rather than the administrators. Let them cease to urge claims which no legislature on earth will yield. Let a senseless and unchristian *plebophobia* be banished from those breasts where it has too long dwelt in moody selfishness. Let them demonstrate to Government, as they well may, the folly of a church without a people, and the utter ineptitude of a Presbyterian Establishment which is not based on the affections of a discerning and attached community."

Men may continue long to differ in their views about the relation of Church and State; but the impartial historian, whatever his views, will never cease to honour, and for ages the devout will continue to draw inspiration from, the courageous faith of those men who, in obedience to their convictions, nearly forty years ago quitted the homes they had made in the parish manses of Scotland. Provost Murray followed his pastor, Dr. Burns, and helped to build up the new church and congregation of Free St. George's in Paisley. The year after the Disruption, 1844, he was elected a deacon; but that was the year of his elevation to the provostship, and of course it was impossible for him, while in that office, to devote much time to the work of the church. On his retirement from the council, however, at the close of his second term in 1850, he was elected an elder, and he became session-clerk in the following year. From that date to the period of his last illness, notwithstanding the numerous and onerous civic duties devolving on him, he spent a good deal of his time in the work of the church, as well as in the promotion of religious and benevolent schemes of a general kind.

It is natural that I should retain especially pleasing recollections of the religious work which he did in his own family. Necessarily this was in a large measure limited to the Sabbath day. It was one of the great sacrifices he had to make in the service of the public, that this was the only day he could ever be sure of spending with his family; and therefore, all through my subsequent life, whenever I have indulged in pictures of home with my father in our midst, imagination always gathers us round the parlour fire on the evening of the sacred day. The pleasing pictures of those old Sabbaths, which I have thus retained, owe very much of their bright colouring to the principles by which my father was guided in the observance of the day. Recognising the sacred character of the Sabbath and

deeply impressed with the importance to mankind
of preserving its sacredness, he was at the same time
singularly liberal in his conception of the particular line of conduct by which that sacredness ought to
be recognised. I remember that some of my school-
fellows used to be surprised, some even shocked, at the
liberties which I spoke of having been allowed on Sunday ; and possibly there are some good people in whom
such liberties would excite the same feelings still. But
the result has been that the Sabbath of my early years,
instead of being, as the Sabbath is too often made, a
synonym for all that is gloomy and oppressive to the
spirit of a child, has come to be associated with those
memories which make home a power of goodness and
joy all through life.

Every Sabbath evening my father followed the practice
which was common in Scottish houses before Sunday
schools came into vogue, and which it would be a
calamity were Sunday schools to displace. For an hour
or so the parlour was converted into a Sunday school,
with my father as teacher. As we grew older, and most
of us became Sunday school teachers ourselves, he
gave up the catechetical instruction which he had
adapted to our younger minds, and used to read to us
some expository work, such as Kitto's *Daily Bible Il-*

lustrations, in explanation of the scriptural passage which had formed the lesson of the evening. Later on, as the family became broken up by marriage and other causes, the usual service of family worship formed the sole exercise of the Sabbath evening. In that my father to the last almost uniformly officiated himself, even after I had entered the church. I believe, he was in favour of the principle that the head of a family should be priest in his own house, and should, as a rule, never surrender his priestly functions to any one in his own sphere.

With such an ideal of his religious duties in the family, it may be presumed that he did not accept office as an elder in the church without undertaking its responsibilities. His position as session-clerk obliged him, of course, to be regular in his attendance at meetings of the kirk-session; and as to his scrupulous conscientiousness in the discharge of the duties thus devolving on him, testimony more explicit or more authoritative cannot be desired than that given by the moderator of the session. "For more than twenty years," says Dr. Thomson, "he has held the office of our session-clerk; and our official records bear testimony, not only to his beautiful penmanship, but also to his orderly methods, and his thorough knowledge of ecclesiastical forms and procedure. A few years ago, when his energies were overtaxed by his other labours, I proposed to get him relieved from this part of his work; but he steadfastly declined. Only a few weeks ago, I offered to do the work for him; but instead of consenting to this, he set himself to make up the arrears caused by his long and severe illness. He was one who could not endure that any duty, belonging to him, should be neglected or postponed."*

In connection with the remarks just quoted, it is observed that "the interests, and especially the spiritual interests, of the congregation lay very near his heart; and he grudged no trouble or labour to advance them." He was always ready, I believe, as far he was

---

* *Christ the Resurrection and the Life: a Sermon preached on the occasion of the Death of Provost Murray.* By the Rev. J. Thomson, D.D., p. 20. One reason, which he stated for declining Dr. Thomson's offer, was, that it would not look well to have a different handwriting in the minute-book; and this may be taken as illustrating the artist's pride that he took in his work. He had always a peculiar delight in fine penmanship, and to the last he could, when he chose, produce specimens that had the appearance of being engraved. In his trade, the only work I ever saw him do with his own hand was that of chalking out those signs in written character which used to go out of his workshop, and were often the objects of admiration for their mathematical accuracy and their chaste style.

F

able, to assist his minister in those various ways in
which the co-operation of an elder may be so valuable. The assistance, which he rendered at prayer-
meetings, is especially referred to by Dr. Thomson.
" When he officiated, as he often did, in the devotions
of our prayer-meeting, especially at the admission of
young communicants, it was a great delight to me to
listen to his prayers, so beautifully expressed, so char-
acterised by deep humility and earnestness, and so
indicative of a highly cultured mind." I have heard
others express themselves in similar terms; and to
young elders, and to young ministers as well, who have
not merely to read the prayers of a prescribed liturgy,
but must find appropriate language for guiding the
devotions of a congregation, it may be instructive to
learn that the prayers, which were found to be so
acceptable, were not merely happy suggestions of the
moment, but, as appears from some remains among his
papers, were evidently the fruit of careful premedita-
tion.

The addresses, too, which he occasionally delivered
at prayer-meetings, were carefully prepared. His
general plan, in preparing an address of any kind,
was to jot down a full outline of the course of thought
he intended to follow; in some cases he seems to have

written out the whole as it might be spoken. But even when he adopted the latter plan, what he wrote was commonly used as a mere guide to the order of thought; he seldom cramped himself by the close reading of a manuscript. Among numerous outlines of addresses on a great variety of subjects there are two, evidently intended for a prayer-meeting, which are written out pretty nearly as they may have been delivered. It is unnecessary, and would scarcely be fair, to discuss the merits of these addresses here, though the author's memory would not, I think, suffer in such a discussion ; they are referred to merely as illustrating the kind of conscientiousness which he displayed in the performance of any duties he undertook.

Those who knew Provost Murray from his more public appearances alone, may not have been prepared for the evidence contained in the above facts, that his life was pervaded by a deep religious spirit. The depth of that spirit could be known only by his more intimate friends. While he always took a keen interest in the intelligent discussion of religious questions, and kept himself to a remarkable degree informed about even the higher problems of theological literature, he had no taste for the goody platitudes which pass current in many circles as religious conversation.

He had also too much tact in dealing with his
fellowmen to obtrude religious subjects in circumstances
where he knew that no religious end could be attained;
and it was certainly not in his nature to make uncalled
for protestations of his own religious feelings before the
world. Religion was to him no mere matter of feeling;
it was nothing if it was not an intelligent guidance in
practical life. We may gain some insight into his
conception of religion from a few sentences which he
penned shortly after the visit of Messrs. Moody and
Sankey to Britain. "Somehow," he says, "I never
could get myself interested in the revival movement
originated by the American evangelists. I felt that
their manner of stating the truth did not suit me nor
realise my views of the Gospel. Doubtless, there is a
necessity for different modes of stating the truths of
Revelation. Some people are appealed to through the
feelings, others by awakening the moral sense, and
others must be reached through the reason. It was
this consideration that led me never to say anything in
disparagement of the revival movement; for I feel that
we should be glad to hail and encourage every influence
which arouses people from their lethargy and indiffer-
ence to the verities of life. At the same time, I cannot help feeling there is always great danger that the

effect of the usual revival preaching will be evanescent. It is true that we cannot limit the grace of God, and it is also true that many have been led to a renewed and sanctified life by the appeal to the feelings, which is characteristic of revival preaching. Still, I suspect the reason why these movements leave so little permanent result compared with the temporary excitement which accompanies them, is that the moral sense and the reason are not sufficiently appealed to. Besides, it has always appeared to me that they make the Christian life too easy, and conversion to be all in all, either ignoring altogether, or not giving sufficient prominence to, the life-long battle which even the most advanced Christian must fight against the sin in his own heart, and the evils in the world around. Under the warm glow of feeling people are made to believe that they are saved, and they are but indifferently prepared for the self-sacrifice that is required before we can realise the true life which consists in making our ordinary daily business one continued act of worship to God."

The healthy piety expressed in these words makes no needless parade of itself before men. It evidently never entered into the writer's mind to make a show of his religious faith by mere talk. He left it to be shown by the work he did. The Christian life, it appears, was to him a life of devout labour in the great cause in which the Master's life was sacrificed,—the welfare of our fellowmen. With all the depth of his religious spirit, therefore, or rather in consequence of its very depth, he always took a hearty delight in doing secular work, and a heartier delight still in doing it well. He had no sympathy with the spurious pietism of those who do the common work of life imperfectly, if they do not shrink from doing it altogether, and then soothe their consciences by calling God and men to witness that their religious feelings are too tender to bear the rough contact with the world which secular work entails.

It is unnecessary to dwell on the theological opinions of a man who never professed to have made a scientific study of theology; and, at any rate, with such an intensely practical interest in religion as that of Provost Murray, dogmatic views necessarily assume less prominence. As an elder in the Free Church of Scotland, he never of course consciously departed from the main lines of Calvinism, though he had no hesitation in recognising the alterations in the form of religious thought and expression that are necessitated by the development of God's providence in our time. He could not abide that morbid exaggeration of isolated

Calvinistic dogmas, which produces often a monstrosity incompatible not only with the glad tidings of divine love, but even with a respectable code of human morality. It cost him no effort, therefore, to place himself in sympathy with earnest men of other creeds, who could not see precisely as he did on religious questions; and he was ready to derive edification from writers of various schools, even though their teachings did not always harmonise with the Calvinistic rule of faith.

Death of a little Sister—Simultaneous Loss of a Mother and
younger Brother—Wee Davie—Death of eldest Daughter—
Wee Annie.

IT was by honest earnest work in God's
world, such as the preceding chapters
have described, that the religious life of
Provost Murray was in the first instance
developed ; and it was perhaps owing to this that his
piety assumed such a healthy form.   It is true that
man is destined to be made perfect by suffering ; but
it is also true that all labour in the service of others,
as it involves the sacrifice of baser selfishnesses, entails
suffering of a kind, and may therefore suffice to unfold
the perfect graces of the Christian life.   But the ster-
ner discipline, which is specially understood by positive
suffering, seems necessary to the spiritual culture of
the great majority of men.   Probably the darkest trials
of every man form a region of the spiritual life which,
as it must be trodden by himself alone, can never be
penetrated by another ; and even if a glimpse into it

be possible, it still remains too awful to be desecrated by exposure to common gaze. But there are some of the more familiar sufferings of human nature that command a universal sympathy; and those, who are interested in the life of Provost Murray at all, will not be unwilling to dwell on some of the sadder incidents, from which it took its more earnest tone.

One of the earliest events in his home-life that he could remember was a scene of sorrow, which must have sunk deeply into his memory, as he writes about it more than sixty years after :—"My first acquaintance with death was made on occasion of the loss of a little sister, younger than myself, from hooping-cough. I was so young that I have not the slightest recollection of what she was like, nor any remembrance of seeing her alive; but the sight of the little corpse stretched on a table and the black coffin are indelibly imprinted on my memory, as also the weeping of my mother, which was my first introduction to the sorrows of life. I do not remember feeling the loss of my sister, but I was pained to see my mother so deeply moved."

There was also an event in his early manhood, which must have left a solemn impression on his mind,—the death of his mother, followed immediately by that of a younger brother. This lad seems to have

been devoted to his mother with a childlike affection of
such singularly passionate intensity, that his life had
become utterly dependent upon hers.   Her loss
accordingly had the effect either of accelerating some
disease of the heart or of producing some violent disturbance in its action, in consequence of which he was
found lifeless in his bed the morning after her death.
I take it as a striking proof of the impression left on
my father's mind, that, though he was fond of talking
about family history, I never heard him once refer to
this event, and I have learnt only from others the
consternation which it excited in his home.

The light of his own household was also darkened
more than once by the loss of his children.   Among
the earliest scenes of my childhood I can recall the
figure of a little brother, wee Davie, who learnt this
world's joys and sorrows only for two brief years.   I
can see the little fellow still, in very vivid image,
squatted on the floor with a kitten gambolling round,
which used to treat us as if he and I had been
specially created for the function of furnishing amusement to it ; and his gleeful laugh rings at times with
startling distinctness in my memory, though it has
been silent for so many years.   But one of the foes of
childhood,—hooping-cough, if I remember aright,—

made its attack upon him ; and early one morning, as I lay beside my elder brother, I was awakened by the light footstep of my father passing through our room, and by my brother's voice whispering, " John, faither's greetin', and I'm sure wee Davie maun be deid." The little face and voice, which touch even me with sadness still, must have brought many a tear to the eye, and many a solemn thought to the mind, of a father.

It was a happy circumstance, which I have heard my father mention with gratitude, that for about a quarter of a century after this, our home was never shadowed by any sorrow of the same kind. But this prolonged serenity imparted a deeper gloom to the cloud which gathered over the household in the autumn of 1866. The eldest of the family, Helen Steel Clark, had been married in 1854 to Mr. Hugh Smith,—a cousin, by the way, of the poet, Alexander Smith. This marriage was the source of much happiness to all concerned, till the summer of 1866, when very serious anxiety was excited by the state of Mrs. Smith's health. Happily, however, she seemed to recover after a few weeks, and in spite of a relapse all anxiety had in a large measure disappeared, when on the 28th of September, her disease assumed an unex-

pected and irresistible force. A hurried message,
owing to her father's absence from home, scarcely
reached him before it was too late; and he arrived at
her bedside only in time to receive one brief flash of
recognition, one brief look of farewell. Two weeks
after, a letter was handed to me by the postman in
Kingston, Canada,—the first I had ever received from
my father with an edge of mourning. The significance
of the symbol of sorrow I could not surmise till I had
opened the letter and read:—" I have very sad news
to communicate. My dear Helen died last night at a
quarter to nine o'clock. I am so terribly crushed that
I cannot trust myself to either speak or write about
the calamity. . . . . This is the
saddest severest blow that I have ever encoun-
tered, and I feel as if both mother and I would
sink under it. . . . . . . My very heart
is bleeding when I look on her five young children
who have lost what they can never find,—a mother's
care and attention. I can write no more, but I could
not think of allowing to-day's U. S. mail to leave without writing to you."

This and subsequent letters of the period reveal the
struggles of a strong spirit to recover from the crush of
an overwhelming blow, but it was long before he re-

gained his old elasticity. It was evident that, in spite of all his struggles, he was perpetually dragged back in helpless anguish upon the memory of the great blank which had been so suddenly created in his heart. The bitterness of spirit over the loss of a first-born child has long been a type of the most unendurable human sorrows ; and my father's mental state, and even his bodily health for some time showed that no suffering had ever ploughed so deeply, or left traces so solemn, in his soul. There was a touching pathos in the tenderness of all his allusions to the child of whom he had been bereaved. It seemed to me at times as if the daughter, of whom his memory kept sadly dreaming, had become transformed by the refinement of sorrow into the little girl, whose dark eyes first illuminated his home with a new joy of life, and whose pattering footsteps first awakened in his heart the music of a father's love.

I have long wished to tell the story of my little sister Annie ; but even yet I shrink from the task of producing a memorial which could be offered as an adequate tribute to her worth. Born on the 26th of August, 1847, with a delicate constitution, she never knew that exuberant joy of robust health, which generally forms the largest element in the happiness of childhood and youth. But she was one of those sufferers who, in spite of bodily disease, never lose the serenity of their spirits ; and therefore, although her figure was abnormally dwarfed by infirmity, her features added to a natural beauty of outline the still higher charm of a happy contentment and kindliness in their expression,—a charm which continued to light up her face at times, even after it had been worn by suffering into premature age and weariness and care. Accordingly, though she could not join the boisterous sports of other children, her early life was brightened by a quiet mirth which made her presence a perennial source of gladness in the household. Such a fountain of joyous thought and feeling became an unfailing resource for cheering a sickbed, especially if the sufferer was a child ; her ingenious and unwearying tact in the invention of amusements was often marvellous. With such a disposition of contentment she naturally did not waste her time in weak and fruitless wailings over a cruel fate ; she braced herself to the duties which her limited strength enabled her to overtake, so that her life, though one of feeble health, was yet filled with many useful labours. Extensive reading, combined with the teachings of a sorrowful experience, had sharpened her intelligence to an unusual degree,—had

developed the wisdom of womanhood even in her girl-
ish years. She had at the same time that happy humility,—that modest estimate of her worth,—which
prevented her from deeming any useful work beneath
her : she was ready for any lowly household duty, and
took delight in tidying a canary's cage, or keeping account of the petty expenses of home.

Amid a life of such cheerful industry, it is not wonderful
that we should seldom have reflected on the probability
of its short duration. But as she reached the close of her
teens it became evident that her defective vitality was nearly spent. The appetite, which had always been pain-
fully meagre, vanished almost entirely in the winter of
1868-9 : and every artifice of medical science was tried
to supply the strength that nature could give only by a
digestion of which she had become incapable. It was
fortunate for me that I was on a visit to Scotland in
the summer of 1869, and had thus the satisfaction of
being beside her during the last three months of her
life. I had arranged to leave again about the beginning of September, and during the last days of August
my attachment for wee Annie began to assume a
peculiarly solemn tenderness in the prospect of being
obliged to bid her a farewell, which we both knew
must be for ever on this earth. But the end was

nearer than either of us supposed. It came just as the
month of August was closing, about eleven o'clock on
the night of the 31st. The friendly hands, that had
nursed her so long, were arranging all the delicate
adjustments of thoughtful love, to try and impart some
ease to the bed which had long ceased to yield her any
invigorating sleep. But a kindlier Hand was smooth-
ing the pillow for her that night, and preparing for her
a rest which she had long been seeking in vain amid
the restlessness of bodily disease. The dropsy, which
was the natural effect of her long confinement, began
a few days before to exhibit alarming symptoms; and
when the end came, it could be said of her with a sort
of literal truth, that " the waters had come in unto her
soul." For she had scarcely laid her head on the pillow, when under the anguish of suffocation she called
to be lifted up. As soon as she was raised, she said,
" It's all over now ;" and with the words, " I can't see
you, mother," she told us that the world had closed on
her for ever. A few spasmodic struggles of the heart
to beat back the rising tide, and then her head lay
motionless on my breast in a peace that is never to be
disturbed.

The impress of such a life cannot be fully realised,
except by filling in its details as only the memory of

her friends can do. It seemed sometimes as if the quiet cheerfulness, and the resigned contentment with her lot, which made her spirit such a power of happiness to her friends, had grown so spontaneously as almost to detract from her personal merit in their culture. But those rare and rich fruits of the Christian life are never the products of mere good nature ; and the internal toil, through which they were cultivated by Annie, was probably all the harder, certainly all the nobler, that she gave her friends only the fruit to enjoy. The warfare, which had to be carried on in her own spirit before she could bring impatient nature to peace, is revealed in a little note-book, where she has privately jotted down a few hymns and other scraps of religious poetry, from which she was evidently wont to draw strength for the spiritual strife. Take, as a specimen, the hymn beginning—

> " I hoped that with the brave and strong
> My portioned task might lie,
> To toil amid the busy throng
> With purpose pure and high."

These words open out a pathetic view of the battle which had to be fought with natural yearnings that aspired to a career of larger activity than could be entered

G

by her,—a career, the closing of which would be
generally taken as turning life into a complete and
irreparable failure. Even near the end it was evidently
not without a pang of regret that she bade adieu to all
the possibilities which she could imagine in a life of
vigorous health. The last entry in her notebook,—
the only one whose penmanship indicates any failure
in steadiness of nerve,—is a lyric of which the regret
over what might have been forms the refrain, though it
expresses also the triumphant surrender of the will to
the lot which God has actually assigned—

> " It might have been ! There is to all a time
> When Memory's bells ring out a mournful chime,
> When voices from the past whisper within,
> ' It might have been, alas, it might have been.'

> *   *   *   *   *   *

> " Say not, ' It might have been !' God wills it so :
> The cup of joy, or yet the cup of woe,—
> He gives us not one bitter drop to sip,
> But Mercy holds the goblet to the lip.

> " O faithful be thou still, and, weary one,
> The welcome rest will come when all is done,
> The calm from sorrow, sweet release from sin,
> When thou shalt cease to sigh, ' It might have been !' "

A day or two before her death I was reading with her the cxxx. psalm—the psalm which for so many generations has formed the cry of the human spirit *de profundis*. Some remark was made about her being peculiarly able to realise the force of the sixth verse, " My soul waiteth for the Lord more than they that watch for the morning." " Yes," she said, " during the long nights I do weary for the morning ; but I'm not long up till I begin to weary again for the night." It seemed as if this natural expression of her suffering had struck her as an unwarrantable outburst of impatience : she checked herself, and said with a quiet tone of self-reproach, " I'm not afraid to die, but I wish I were more patient." I could not help feeling humbled before the grandeur of the victory which a spirit of resignation had won, when even an utterance of the helpless weariness of nature was repressed as an uprising of an impatient spirit. In that serener life, where bodily strength, like other powers that are merely of the earth, counts for nothing,—where devout service to the divine will counts for all in all,—we shall find in the sublime spiritual energies of many a resigned sufferer an illus-tration of Milton's great words—

" They also serve who only stand and wait."

That such a life and such a death should have produced a profound effect on a father's mind, is a mere matter of course; and Annie's father has left a very full record of the sacred affection with which he cherished her memory. No one can feel astonished that, on the day after her death, he should have written:—"Another of the lights of my earthly existence is extinguished. . . . . . . I never loved any child so tenderly. I could not help it; she was such a treasure of goodness in a house. Her gentle child-like nature, her tender attachment and great good sense endeared her to me; and her long illness made my attachment one of the tenderest I have ever enjoyed. I do not recollect ever having had occasion to reprove her; and at such a season as this how pleasing the thought, that memory cannot recall a single unpleasant word having ever passed between us!

"It has been my wont for some time past, before leaving for business, to go out into the garden, and cut a few fresh flowers, to present to her in her sick-room; and she greatly appreciated the simple gift. I went this morning to cut the flowers, but, alas! only to lay them on that breast, now cold, that used to cherish toward me such loving regard. My dearest wee Annie, does thy pure and guileless spirit look down even now on thy sorrowing father? I feel as if thy departure has added another link—a golden link—to attach me to that home, to which thou hast gone before."

VIII.—SECOND PERIOD OF PUBLIC SERVICE.

Appointed Collector of Inland Revenue for Renfrewshire and
Buteshire, and afterwards for Argyleshire—Elected to the
Town Council and the Provostship—The Burgh acquires
the Gasworks, recovers from Insolvency, and obtains an Improvement Bill—Provost Murray's character as an Adminis-
trator.

IT was shortly after the loss referred to in
the latter part of the previous chapter, that
Provost Murray returned to the council of
his native town. His return to public
office was unexpected,—had never been spoken of
even a few weeks before. He had rendered a long and
arduous service to the town during the most trying
period of its history. He had occupied the office of
chief magistrate during two terms, so that there was no
higher municipal honour which he could receive. His
townsmen had recognised the unusual length and
value of his services by the presentation of a handsome
testimonial on the occasion of his retirement in 1850.

We have seen also that, though no longer a member of the town council, he continued to find numerous occupations of another sort in the service of the community. In 1869, moreover, when he was asked to enter into municipal office again, he was passing the prime of life, and might have been excused if he had shrunk from such an addition to his work. To explain his acceptance of office under all these circumstances there may have been many minor reasons. Among these perhaps the most influential was the fact that he now enjoyed more leisure than he had during his earlier public career. In 1862, he had been appointed to the office of Collector of the Inland Revenue and Distributor of Stamps for the counties of Renfrew and Bute. To the work of this office, indeed, he gave a great deal more of personal superintendence than is probably common among collectors ; and the result was that the accuracy and efficiency of the system which he introduced were more than once made the subject of special recognition at headquarters, and led to his undertaking, at the Comptroller-general's request, the additional duties of the Argyle-shire office. Still the labour thus entailed on him was far from implying the incessant and anxious strain of a private business ; and it is not surprising that he

should have felt himself in the enjoyment of a leisure
which justified him in undertaking again important
public duties.   But though this and other reasons may
have had some influence in determining him to accept
municipal office at this time, I believe his predominating
motive was the desire to retrieve the calamities which
had overwhelmed the town during his previous connection with the council ; and evidently no event of his
public life afforded him a more sincere gratification
than the attainment of this object.

It has been already pointed out that, in order to
the recovery of the town, a complete alteration of its
industries was required.   This change had been slowly
going on since the time of its disasters.   Various new
industries had sprung into existence ; and some of the
old manufactures, like that of thread after the invention
of the sewing machine, had grown to unexpected
dimensions.   This revival of prosperity was gradually
accumulating a new wealth, which promised a gratifying
improvement in the commercial credit of the municipality ; and men of public spirit began to inquire
whether an attempt should not be made to restore the
burgh to a position of solvency.   A premature attempt
of this kind had been made in 1855 under the provostship of Mr. Hugh Macfarlane.   In the promotion of

this measure Provost Murray co-operated earnestly with his successor. The bill which they endeavoured to carry through parliament does credit to the intelligence of its promoters, as well as to their judicious consideration for the interests of all concerned ; and it seems now difficult to understand why it should have been opposed.

The interval, however, between 1855 and 1869 had undoubtedly put the town in a much more favourable position for making an amicable settlement with its creditors, and all that was wanted was a man with sufficient knowledge of the town's affairs, with sufficient energy and leisure, to carry out the scheme. An example had just been set of a former provost returning to the civic chair for the purpose of rendering a service which demanded more judicious management than could be generally expected from an inexperienced official. Provost Macfarlane had just carried out a scheme, involving serious expenditure, for providing a vast addition to the water-supply of the town ; and he had the satisfaction of accomplishing this without increasing the water-rates of the inhabitants. If he had remained in office, he would doubtless have been able to continue his work of improvement in other directions ; but he had seen it his duty to retire from the magis-

tracy in 1869, before his term had expired. The
gratifying result experienced from obtaining the services of a tried official, seems to have suggested a re-
newal of the experiment; and with surprising unani-
mity the thoughts of the electors settled on Provost
Murray, who had often before been closely associated
with Provost Macfarlane in municipal affairs. On being requested to offer himself as a candidate, Provost
Murray gave his consent on condition that he should
be relieved from the necessity of canvassing; but the
friends, at whose solicitation he acted, showed that they
had estimated popular sentiment aright. He was elected to the council, and then into the provost's chair,
without opposition.

The measure, to which the provost first gave his
attention, was one which he had just before urged on
the consideration of his townsmen. The manufacture
of gas in general, and especially for the use of his
native town, was always a subject of interest to him.
When he began to study chemistry in Dr. M'Kechnie's
Surgery, the practicability of using carburetted hydro-
gen for general lighting was a favourite topic among
the new applications of science; and I have often
heard him speak of the first experiments made in the
town very much as a young enthusiast of the present

day may tell fifty years hence about the experiments now being made with the electric light.

He had, therefore, always taken more or less of a practical interest in the gasworks of Paisley. The company, by whom the works were built, had secured a monoply of the gas-supply under certain conditions, one of which was that the burgh should be at liberty to purchase the property whenever that might be deemed advisable in the public interest. Some progress had been already made in the purchase of the gas-company's stock. Provost Murray had explained in a pamphlet the previous history and the existing state of the relation between the municipality and the company. He now urged that the purchase of the property should be completed, and the entire management of the gas-works assumed by the town council in the interest of the community. He had the satisfaction of carrying this measure within a few months after his return to office; and the town thus entered into the enjoyment of two very indispensable requisites of comfortable living,—a plentiful supply both of water and light at unusually cheap rates.

Immediately after this the provost broached his scheme for terminating the trust, under which, since its bankruptcy, the estate of the burgh had been held on behalf of its creditors, and reinvesting the town council in the control of the estate. The details of this measure, though not without value as an economical and political study, can scarcely be of interest except to those who have some associations with Provost Murray or with his native town; and they are already sufficiently acquainted with the subject. For this reason also it is unnecessary to enter into a detailed account of Provost Murray's municipal administration during this period; it will be sufficient to notice another measure of special importance, with which his name is associated.

In consequence of the financial condition of the burgh, it had been found impossible to accomplish many improvements in the way of widening streets, drainage, &c., which had long become necessary. But this difficulty had been overcome by the burgh re-acquiring the management of its own estate. The gasworks also had turned out a very valuable property, yielding a large surplus even after supplying a superior quality of gas at an exceedingly low rate. With the funds thus placed at the disposal of the town council a scheme of improvement was planned, and a bill based on it passed through parliament in 1877. The result is that the next few years will see greater alterations in the general aspect of Paisley than have taken place for nearly half a century before; and possibly the town may thus be invested with an amenity, which it seems to lack in the eyes of strangers.*

One of the most important facts connected with the three measures just described is that they were all carried through parliament without opposition. This seems a very simple statement; but probably no one, except the originator of the measures, knows all that it implies. Every one of course knows that it implies the saving of very large sums in legal expenses, as well as the avoidance of those unpleasantnesses, which are usually excited by municipal conflicts in such cases, and which often imperil the success of a measure even after it has become law. But few, who have not tried the task, can realise the amount of labour which it cost

---

* When the provost was in London, carrying his Improvement Bill through parliament, he was explaining its provisions one day to a lady who had been born in Paisley, but who, on revisiting her native town, after spending some years under serener skies, had been somewhat shocked by its dingy streets. "Dear me, provost!" she exclaimed at last, assuming for fun her native *patois*, "I wonner ye gie yoursel' sae muckle bother aboot improvin' sic a like place. The only way to improve 't is tae ding 't doon!"

to get all opposition removed before making an application to parliament. Provost Murray's success in this respect had its source in various features of his intellectual and moral character. He was gifted undoubtedly with unusual tact in dealing with others in private as well as in public ; but this gift was itself a combination of various powers. It implied of course considerable knowledge of human nature. But that knowledge is unhappily often combined in administrators with a concealment which frequently amounts to deception. Most men are weak enough to be tempted into the delusion that great ends can be reached more cleverly than by the open road of truthfulness which the Almighty has prescribed; only the few have the intellectual and moral qualification to be

" Mildly secure in power that knows no guile."

Provost Murray seemed to follow, as if by a fine instinct, the method of perfect frankness in all transactions with his fellowmen, especially as a servant of the people. Having entered public life without any selfish object in view, he never had any motive for concealment, any purpose to be attained by diplomatic trickery. Accordingly throughout his career he preserved a reverent attachment to constitutional forms of procedure; for constitutional liberty and constitutional order are based on that regard for the rights of others, which scorns the seduction to seek a political object by circumvention. It is a striking proof of this, that, with all his pronounced liberalism, he yet retained to a large extent the confidence of local conservatives. They knew he embodied that fine constitutional sense, which prevents a man from straining legal processes in order to carry a pet scheme; they knew that, however ardently he might desire a measure of reform, he would never try to force it on the community until the community had been induced to demand it in a constitutional way. But all this had a deeper source in him than mere speculative opinion; theories in political science, however favourable to constitutional liberty, are apt to break down under the pressure of the passions evoked in political conflicts. They require to be sustained by the habit of doing to others as we would have others do to us. Only in this sacred disposition to recognise the claims of others is there any security for social freedom and order; but with this disposition freedom and order are tolerably secure under any political system.

An additional source of Provost Murray's success in

dealing with others is to be found in the conscientious labour which he bestowed on any service he undertook. During his public life he had of course made himself familiar with the history, the constitution, the difficulties and the requirements of his native town ; so that his pamphlets, his speeches, his conversational explanations generally succeeded in giving a delusive appearance of simplicity to a really complicated scheme. His power of luminous exposition was very remarkable in reference to minute and even intricate details. A crowd of facts, which in most hands would run into perplexing chaos, could be marshalled by him in an intelligible order which made all point to the conclusion they were intended to enforce. A conspicuous example of this power is the speech with which he introduced to the council his measure for recovering the burgh from insolvency. Another example I remember on one of those occasions on which he appeared as a witness for a bill before a committee of the House of Commons. At the very opening of the case it became evident that the counsel conducting the examination had not had time to master his brief. A few questions, however, showed him that the witness was familiar with the case in its minutest details. The counsel had therefore the good sense to allow the witness to proceed of his own accord, so that the examination passed into an address of about three hours interrupted only by an occasional inquiry from a member of the committee.

Mr. David Gilmour has furnished me with an additional illustration :—" Provost Murray astonished me on one occasion by his mastery of details. He had been appointed sole referee on a case which had passed through several hands for settlement unsuccessfully ; and as it referred to yarns and webs, he requested me to spend half-an-hour in his back-shop, which I did, and answered a few questions. The day following he called at my office, and read his decision, which embodied *all* my answers, and connected them in such a common-sense way, as not only astonished me at his grasp of technical details, but gave satisfaction to both parties in the dispute."

It may have been owing to this power of mastering the details of a scheme, that he was so often called to give evidence before parliamentary committees. His appearance there in connection with private bills from the North had become so familiar, that Lord Redesdale is said to have on one occasion humorously dubbed him " the provost of Scotland." Perhaps it was this power also, combined with his scrupulous impartiality, and his generous readiness to help others, that led to his being so frequently consulted as a referee in business disputes. These cases often entailed upon him a vast amount of labour. In fact the secret of all lucid speaking and writing, of all lucid decisions in the complications of justice, is a very open secret. It is found in the pains bestowed upon a subject by the man who undertakes to make it clear to his fellowmen. Provost Murray seemed to find a pleasure in such pains. But all my previous knowledge of his habits had not prepared me for the evidence, which his papers furnished, of the elaborate calculations, the extensive correspondence, the lengthy, and sometimes far from pleasant, interviews with all sorts of people, which represent his labours for the community.

Of all this, however, it is needless to say, he was never heard to complain, he would have been the last man to dream of complaining. Unselfish toil had become the habit of his life. Doubtless he felt a justifiable pride in the repeated confidence which his townsmen had placed in him, as well as in the honourable position in which their confidence sustained him so long. Certainly the appreciation of his public labours was such as does not often fall to the lot of public men. Few men, who have occupied a prominent position so long in any community, have escaped so

clean from the filth of malicious slander which is apt
to be flung wildly about by the heedless passions of
municipal war. Any unjustifiable utterances, that may
have been spoken against Provost Murray, were such
as his most enthusiastic friends can readily afford to
forget. His repeated re-election to his honourable
office proved that his townsmen thoroughly appreciated
his worth. All this generous appreciation was undoubtedly a source of satisfaction ; but beyond this
honest gratification he desired no earthly reward. He
had a singular tenderness in shrinking from any action
which might be misinterpreted as indicating mercenary
motives in the work he did for others. Indeed some
of his friends used to think him almost Quixotic in the
scruples which led him to decline perquisites, and even
reimbursements, which perhaps, for the sake of the
community itself, ought to have been accepted.

A hale Old Age—Moderation of Character—Genial Kindliness—
The Clique—The Old Man among his children and grandchildren.

THE enthusiasms of literature have been
kindled not merely by the fires of youth
and manhood's prime; the calmer warmth
and the more luminous glow of age have
found their admirers too. Notwithstanding the high
pressure of modern civilisation there are still not a few
among us who wisely husband their resources so that
they are able to enjoy a hearty interest in life even
after the passions of youth have died out. Provost
Murray was one of those. No one could come in
contact with him during the last few years of his life
without feeling himself in presence of a man thoroughly
hale in body and in soul. One of the complimentary
commonplaces of his townsmen during these years
consisted in genial allusions to the juvenility of thought
and feeling which he retained in his advancing age.

One expression of this nature may be cited, as it called from the provost a remark which seemed to indicate for the first time a consciousness that his work was coming to a close. At a luncheon given on the 21st of October, 1878, at the opening of the new Seedhill Bridge,—one of the earliest fruits of the Improvement Bill,—Mr. P. Comyn Macgregor made some kindly and graceful allusions to "the ever-green and perpetual provost." The reply, after an introductory expression of thanks, went on :—"All I can say is, and it is a confession which I think you will give me credit for—as it is forty-two years since I entered the town council, though I had a rest of nineteen years during that period, and you are all witnesses to the amount of time and labour which I have bestowed on public affairs during the last nine years ;—that, after my long services, whether it is the feeling of the community or not, there is a feeling creeping over myself, that, to use the language of the poet,—

'Superfluous lags the veteran on the stage.'"

The remark was immediately met by cries of No, No ; and the provost, evidently touched by the generous reception, was induced to add that, "whether he remained in the town council or not, he would cherish · the deepest feelings of gratitude for the respect and courtesy and support which he had received at all times from his fellow-townsmen whilst endeavouring to do their work." But in the light of the following half-year one can almost interpret his words as an indication that a vague feeling of decaying strength was already beginning to appear.

His private duties were considerably increased during the last few years of his life by his undertaking, in 1872, the management of a branch of the Royal Bank of Scotland, which was opened in Paisley at that time.* On the occasion of this appointment he tendered his resignation of the collectorship of the Inland

---

* "It is a curious coincidence," my father writes, " that Mr. David Dale was the first agent of the Royal Bank in Glasgow, which was opened in 1783, close upon ninety years before I opened the first agency of the Royal Bank in Paisley. When Mr. Dale was appointed to the bank agency, he was carrying on business as an importer of Flanders yarn in a small shop in High Street, five doors north of the cross. He paid £5 of rent; but, thinking this an extravagant sum, he had sublet one half to a watchmaker for 50s. In 1783, when he was appointed agent for the bank, the watchmaker's half of the shop was turned into the bank-office." See Strang's *Glasgow and its Clubs*, p. 300.

Revenue; but, at the request of the Comptroller-general, he was induced to continue his superintendence of the office. The arrangement was not of the most satisfactory kind on the whole. The emoluments of the office, which had never been an excessive remuneration for the work performed, were to a large extent absorbed by the additional subordinates who had to be employed; while the responsibility was seriously increased by the necessity of leaving the work so much to others. It is but fair to add, however, that the collector was relieved of many anxieties by the confidence which he was always able to repose in the efficiency and conscientiousness of the gentleman who had charge of the head-office of the district in Greenock.

It appears, therefore, that the private, as well as the public, life of Provost Murray, during its closing years, was filled with a manifold activity. But, laborious though it was thus rendered, his old age, during its brief duration, was one of unusual serenity. This was largely, if not altogether, due, as in all such cases it must be, to the character of his previous life. His general character was prominently marked by what is properly called moderation or temperance in the largest sense of the term. There are two groups of passions which chiefly require moderation, as being

most inimical to the higher welfare of man.   These
are those passions of our animal nature which manifest
themselves in the various forms of sensual vice, and
those unsocial passions whose excessive indulgence
leads to envy, malice, and all uncharitableness.
Provost Murray could not have been the unselfish worker
for others that he was, if he had not been endowed, in a
large measure, with that cultured self-control which
moderates both these tendencies of human nature.

One of these forms of self-control has been already
remarked in Provost Murray : he was gifted with a
peculiarly placid temper.   It is worthy of mention that
one of his earliest literary efforts is a paper in a local
periodical called *The Tickler*, bearing the somewhat
unpromising title of *The Lucubrations of Nicholas
Novum, Gentleman*, which contains what, for a young
man, are some very wise observations on the importance
to human happiness of that generous regard for the
feelings of others, which forms the soul of real good
nature and of all true courtesy.   This invaluable attri-
bute of human character was undoubtedly, as has been
already observed, one source, perhaps the chief source,
of that peculiar tact in dealing with others, that perfect
openness, that love of constitutional order, to which
mainly he owed his success in the administration of

public business. It was also the source of many of
those enjoyments which contributed to the serenity of his
later years. Having spent his whole life in the place
in which he had been born and brought up, he had the
opportunity of forming some of those friendships which
take a richer aroma from their age. It is not lack of
opportunity alone that allows to men so few of those
blessings; our intercourse is too often soured by a
temper which may neutralise all the sweetness of early
affection. The friendships that last through life, are,
therefore, usually to be regarded as indicative of a
peculiarly genial bearing on the part of those by whom
they are sustained. Among my father's old friends
there was a circle of some half-a-dozen couples, who
were wont to take a round of quiet festivities at each
other's houses during winter, and in summer an "out-
ing" or two at one of the remoter watering-places
where they could enjoy a picnic. In consequence of
the peculiar exclusiveness of this circle, which was the
frequent subject of a pleasant jest among outsiders, it
came to be familiarly dubbed *the clique*,—a name given
originally, I believe, in good humour by the youngsters
of the families, though accepted in as good humour by
the old folks. I cannot reflect on the long existence
of this kindly association among old friends without

feeling that it must have been the source of many un-
alloyed enjoyments to them all, and perhaps also—

> " Of that best portion of a good man's life,—
> His little nameless, unremembered acts
> Of kindness and of love."

One of the members of this pleasant circle, and one
of my father's oldest friends, was ex-Provost Brown.
He probably disclosed the link which bound this knot
of friends together for such a length of time, when he
assured me that his long companionship with my
father had never been marred by a single unpleasant
incident.   This assurance is all the more creditable to
both provosts, as they were of different political stripe,
and had generously agreed to differ on some other
points as well.

It was not among his old friends alone, that Provost
Murray showed his attractive bearing : those, whose
intimacy was more recent and of briefer duration, felt
the same attraction.   In illustration of this it is with
great pleasure that I am able to quote the following
generous letter from Professor Macgregor, formerly of
the Free High Church in Paisley :—

New College, Edinburgh,
16th March, 1880.

" My Dear Murray,

"An opportunity of speaking
to the world about your father is most grateful to me.
I once had a newspaper controversy with him, which
certainly did not lead me to cherish wrath. Like all
the really manly men whom I have met, he was simple
and candid. In his case this was remarkable, because
his life was in a large measure a life of skilled administration; and skilled administrators often find it
necessary to put on a false face. . . . .
. . . . . He therefore had occasion for Scottish
'pawkieness.' And he had, in a high degree that rare
species of prudence which enables a man to avoid needless friction while going on to his own ends with force-
ful determination. But, most rare in anyone, and
most admirable in him, he was the very soul of can-
dour.

"To Paisley he was a great citizen. To the west of
Scotland he was a great politician. To the Free Church
he was a veritable tower of strength. And to the
Christian cause he was wholly devoted, his whole life
being quietly effective for the highest end, not only in
his own denomination, but in the community as a
whole.

" Looking back and recalling to mind and heart his
fine face and noble figure, I feel what a *friend* he was,
even to those who were not in the close intimacy of

every day fellowship with him. On my rare visits to
Paisley after being called to Edinburgh, my heart
always drew to 'the provost's' house. He must have
been very affectionate, though very undemonstrative.
My wife tells me that, immediately after my election
to the chair I now occupy, there was a loud knock at
our door in Paisley, followed by the question, 'Is the
professor at home?' Delicate and considerate kind-
ness was characteristic of your father.

"It will hardly be believed that a man, who took so
great a place in municipal and political business, was
a keen student of the highest literature. I have more
than once been astonished by the juvenile _freshness_ of
your father's interest in purely speculative questions.
He had the rare happiness of retaining his youth to his
old age.

"The first occasion of my seeing him was a meeting
of a conference of Paisley office-bearers of various
denominations. I then and there read a paper on the
church's relation to her young members, as represented
by the baptism of infants. There was a good deal of
twaddle talked. But a man with a fine face and noble
figure had taken in the young minister's view, and proposed that the paper should be printed for the godly
instruction and stimulation of all office-bearers. That
was my first close view of 'the provost.'

"The _quietness_ of Provost Murray's force is what
strikes one most on looking back. In Paisley he could
do almost what he liked. But he had 'the kingly

governing faculty.' His own likings he did not indulge to the extreme of egotism. He waited until people were ready to take advice from one who, partly by his patient waiting, had come to have a sensible right to advise.

"Your father's mind was fine and high. His temper was sweet and generous. He was 'a nobleman by creation of God Almighty.' He was a Christian in profession and in practice. If Principal Dawson and you and others in authority at Montreal come to be such men as Provost Murray was, the Queen will have cause to rejoice on behalf of the Dominion.

Yours truly,
JAMES MACGREGOR."

It appears as if even casual acquaintances found in their passing intercourse with Provost Murray a certain charm of intelligent kindliness. I have often been struck by the terms in which my personal friends on both sides of the Atlantic, who paid him occasional visits or even a single brief call, used to speak of their genial reception ; and at the time of his death there was a melancholy sort of gratification in the numerous letters of condolence from men who had been comparative strangers, but retained grateful recollections of a little friendly intercourse with him, as well as of his work for the people. "I cannot help sending you a line or two," writes a friend to the Rev. Dr. Thomson, "to say how much I sympathise with you in your new sorrow. It is not every congregation that has a Provost Murray to lose ; and when such a one is taken away, his minister and fellow-members must feel doubly bereaved ; they lose a personal friend of rare worth, and an office-bearer whose loss seems, at least for the time, to be irreparable. . . . . I cannot account for being so much drawn to him, when I consider how little altogether was my personal intercourse with him. There must have been about him that sort of rich aroma of genuine goodness which makes itself quickly, though indescribably felt."*

But how shall I describe the subtle charm of goodness, when to the patient kindliness of his general manner was added the tenderness of fatherly and grandfatherly love? It has often been said that men live a second life in their children. I have often thought that my father found this proverbial saying realised rather as his grandchildren grew up around him. It has been already mentioned that one of the great sacrifices, which he made in the service of the com-

---

* *Sermon preached on the Occasion of the Death of Provost Murray.* By the Rev. J. Thomson, D.D., pp. 18, 19.

munity, arose from the fact that his public duties prevented him from enjoying, as he might have done, the
associations of his own home. In his later life he
found, to an extent that had been denied him before,
an opportunity of indulging those parental gratifications which give a fresh, and perhaps a purer, taste of
the joys that pass away with our early years. Nothing
could surpass the self-sacrificing care with which he
followed his children into the new sphere of their own
homes, and exceeded even them in patient concern for
their little ones. It was often a mystery to me when
I saw him with his grandchildren, how his spirit could
so lightly leap the chasm between his age and their in-
fancy, rejoicing with childlike heartiness in their simple joys, and patiently soothing their little griefs. Even
during the last days of his illness the severe suffering
which he endured at times, did not drive from his
mind the thought of a little grandson who had been
prevented from competing for prizes at school by a
prolonged absence rendered necessary on account of
sickness at home. On the day on which the prizes
were distributed, he had the boy brought to his bedside ; and after some words of affectionate sympathy
and encouragement, he made him a handsome pre-

sent by way of compensation for the prizes that might have been gained.

But after all is there any mystery is this sympathetic attraction of childhood and age? Is not the secret to be found in the fact that the little ones found in their grandfather the character, which was felt by all with whom he came into contact,—of one to whom the thought of self came last, to whom the first thought was that of doing what is right and kindly towards every human being, young or old, rich or poor alike? Was it any wonder, therefore, that his presence among us was like an external conscience, for ever uttering its silent but powerful reproof against all selfishness, against all tendency to grow weary in well-doing for the good of others?

It is natural that I should cherish peculiarly vivid and peculiarly tender reminiscences of the affection which has followed me since I left the old home in 1862. The patient labour, which my father was always ready to spend upon others, was never more strikingly exhibited than in his untiring thoughtfulness about our distant home. A mail was never allowed to pass without some communication from him. The local papers were almost uniformly addressed to me in his own handwriting, and they were almost always accompanied

by a letter of considerable length. His letters to his
children were peculiarly fine; they were, indeed, so
charmingly adapted to their purpose—so full of gossip
about the persons and events in whom his correspon-
dents were interested—that they could seldom be of
any interest to others. Perhaps the only exception to
this was in his letters to me, which occasionally retailed
such literary, political, or ecclesiastical gossip as had
come in his way, and as he thought might possibly not
reach a colony.

But it was on our visits from Canada that I recall the
most memorable manifestations of his affectionate
nature. It seemed as if his love for the distant members of his family circle, having been pent up during
the long years of their absence, had to find vent during
the brief weeks of their visit; and it consequently
gushed out with an intensity which can never be forgotten by those on whom it was lavished. Our last
visit in 1877 is peculiarly memorable, not only because
it was crowded with scenes of social happiness, but because he has left a record, which will be referred to
presently, of the impression it left on his own mind.
My children were old enough to enter into the general
prattle that passed around the table; and their Canadian manners and accent and dialect, which were a

I

perpetual source of merriment to their Scotch cousins,
attracted often his kindly interest and kindly observa-
tion.   At one time he might be seen sitting amid a
batch of grandchildren who filled up one of the bay-
windows in the Bank House, while an occasional funny
smile indicated the zest with which he watched the
fresh wonder of the Canadians at the novel sights
passing along the crowded streets, and listened to the
unfamiliar forms of speech in which their wonder was
expressed.   At another time the youngsters were to be
seen squatted on the floor in every imaginable attitude
around his chair, while some one led them in " Ten
Little Nigger Boys," or some equally boisterous rhyme.
Or a number of them came scampering after us, as he
and I sallied out to some part of the town or suburbs,
where he wished to show me some alterations that had
been going on since I was last there.   On the Sabbath
evenings he took a special pleasure in talking about
the peculiar modes of worship, the favourite hymns,
the means of Sunday school tuition, and other facts in
the active life of the Canadian Churches.   And it is
with a sacred pathos that I recall the look of serene
satisfaction, with which he listened to his grandchildren from the other side of the sea singing to him,
before they went to bed, a simple evening hymn which

they had been taught by their French-Canadian
nurse :—

> " Je suis las, il fait nuit ;
>   Bon soir, cher petit père ;
>   Couche moi, bonne mère,
> Porte moi dans mon lit.

> " Redis moi ma prière :—
>   Bon Dieu, veille sur moi ;
>   Fais moi vivre pour toi,
> Pour mon père et ma mère."

X.—THE END.

N the 22nd of August, 1877, my father wrote :—"My son John, with his wife and two children, has been with me on a visit for the past three months. They leave us again to-morrow to return to Montreal. Parting with dear friends, who are to be separated by so great a distance, and for that reason for a long period of time, is always painful. My wife and I are looking forward to our parting to-morrow with feelings of more sadness than on any former occasion, from a consciousness that at our ages the probability is very great, that to one of us, if not both, this may be a final parting, and that we may never meet again on this side of time."

On reading these words after my father's death, they naturally recalled the incident of our parting the even-

ing after they were written. I was somewhat struck
myself by the unusual fervour in the grasp of his hand;
but a few hours after, as we steamed down the Clyde,
on our way to overtake the s.s. *Sardinian* at London-
derry, my wife remarked that my father had never
parted from her in that manner before; his embrace
had been like that of one who felt that he might never
see her again. Still there was nothing for a long time
to indicate that this sentiment was other than one of
those baseless forebodings which pass out of memory
when they are unverified by subsequent events. Up
to the Spring of 1879, we continued to cherish the intention of visiting the old place again in 1880, to cele-
brate the golden wedding of my father and mother.
There was every prospect of his enjoying some years
of vigorous activity, and even of his being spared to an
advanced old age. But, unfortunately, men of constitutional energy, who find pleasure in ceaseless occupation, are often tempted to take dangerous liberties,
such as are scrupulously avoided by those whose
feebler strength demands perpetual care in order to
the preservation of health. All his life long, but
especially during his prime, Provost Murray was apt,
under the pressure of public and private business, to
be negligent of those simple laws in reference to

regularity of meals, upon which the general health, as requiring healthy digestion, depends. Whether this was the cause of the disease which proved fatal, it is unnecessary to discuss; certainly it was the digestive apparatus that broke down. Symptoms of disorder made their appearance in 1878; and all during the winter of 1878-9, he suffered spasms of indigestion, which, it now seems astonishing, should not have led to more decided measures for the preservation of his life. But no symptoms of a definite disease were noticed till the spring had pretty far advanced. He had been with my father-in-law in London about the beginning of March, giving evidence before a committee of the House of Commons on some bill connected with the harbour of Renfrew. The weather was unusually severe at the time, and he returned with a cold caught either in the metropolis or on the journey home.

For two or three weeks after this journey, he was annoyed in the morning with a cough, and his meals were almost uniformly followed with the burning acidity of indigestion. Like other men who have enjoyed vigorous health throughout life, he could not easily be made to feel the necessity of subjecting himself to the restraints of an invalid; and accordingly the symptoms of disorder, from which he was suffering, failed to bring him the warning they implied. He continued, therefore, in the discharge of his public as well as his private duties with an assiduity which was very unwise in view of its effect, however creditable on account of its motive. On the 23rd of March he performed even an official act which is a useless, though picturesque, relic of a former state of things. It was an ancient custom of the magistrates of Paisley, as of many other places, to "redd the marches" of the town by walking round them every year. The provost, with all his reforming zeal, had a sentiment for the antique, which grew, naturally, with the mellowing influences of age. Accordingly, he started on this needless ramble with his colleagues; but it was an indication of his failing strength, that he was obliged to sit down and rest at one point, where they made a *détour* and returned for him. The imprudence of this unnecessary fatigue and exposure was admitted by himself on coming home; and such an admission from him contained a very significant proof of the injurious effect which it had produced.

From this time his health steadily deteriorated. Occasionally a strange look of painful weariness came over his face, and alarmed those who were most interested in his welfare; but there was no symptom of illness decided enough to induce him to seek medical advice. On the 6th of April he officiated as an elder at the communion service, though he felt far from well; but he was unable to go back to church in the evening. It was just a fortnight after, on the 21st of April, that a change first became noticeable in the colour of his skin. Two days afterwards it was evident that he had taken jaundice. It is now, of course, impossible to say whether the disease might not have been arrested if the necessary precautions had been taken from the moment when it became pronounced. But it was singularly unfortunate that the very day on which the jaundice was unmistakable,—the 23rd of April,—was that fixed for the election of the School Board. Having been appointed Returning-Officer, he was so rigidly conscientious in discharging the duties of the position that he remained with the clerks till the late hour at which the ballots were counted, and then went out into the cold night air, and announced the results to the assembled crowd. Even for two days after the election he did not begin to treat himself as an invalid; but by that time—perhaps, indeed, long before that—the disease had got beyond the control of human skill.

His strong constitution yielded slowly to the attack. It was more than three months before the struggle closed. After a while it was found impossible in town to get exercise conveniently in the fresh air, and it was suggested that he should retire for a little to the country. This led to his residence for a few weeks at Kilmalcolm. Unhappily, the weather was extremely unfavourable for any advantage to be gained from the fine air of th's retreat. That was the year in which, the historian of our own times has recently remarked, there was "practically no summer."* The result was that he felt so little benefited by the change, that he began to weary again for home; and his return was followed for a few days by such an agreeable effect upon his spirits, that he even went down once or twice to his office in the bank. At the beginning of July the disease reached a crisis; and from that time little hope of his recovery was possible, except during an interval of some ten days, when he enjoyed a comparative relief from suffering, though he made no advance towards a cure.

But after all the mere course of a disease is of little

---

* M'Carthy's "History of our own Times," chap. lxvi.

interest to any but the scientific student of medicine. The friend of Provost Murray is more concerned to know the current of his inner life during this unusual and unwelcome disaster of the outward man. From the first moment when he found himself compelled to submit to careful medical treatment, he addressed his mind to the stern, but wholesome schooling which affliction brings. At an early stage of his disease, on the 6th of May, he writes :—" I have been confined to the house for twelve days from indisposition, I cannot say that I feel any improvement of my health up to this time. My medical advisers assure me that as yet there is no organic disease, but only functional derangement : still I feel that this attack of jaundice is the culmination of a long-continued derangement of the digestive organs. In consequence of this and of my advanced age I fear that the prospects of recovery are not so great. I have a good constitution, however, and that may help to carry me through this illness, though I can scarcely hope to be ever so strong and healthy as I have been. I have observed in the case of many old men who have, like myself, enjoyed a long and uninterrupted course of good health, that the first break-down is the final one. Whether this is the beginning of the end with me, I cannot and must not attempt to predict. I must just wait the issue with patience, and bow with reverent submission to the will of my Heavenly Father.

"I have great reason to be deeply thankful to that Heavenly Father for the long course of unbroken health which I have enjoyed. I seek now to realise that He never afflicts willingly or without a purpose of mercy any of His children, and that this illness may, in His great love, be an exercise of His moral discipline to bring me back to Himself, and draw me closer to the Saviour. For I do feel that the too heavy and engrossing cares of public and private business have so absorbed my attention as to leave me too little time for communion with God or for reflection on the great change that, whether now or not, cannot be long distant.

"I am thankful that I have been enabled, in some measure, to profit by my present illness, for I feel, as I have never felt before, the preciousness of Christ. I have often vainly attempted to construct a logical theory of the atonement—its nature, conditions, and extent. I now feel the rest and satisfaction of a simple, child-like faith in the Lord Jesus. There are many things in the world and in man, regarding which I cannot satisfy my reason. Life itself is a mystery. The

communication of mind to mind is equally mysterious;
and need I wonder that the great mystery of godliness
—God manifest in the flesh—is beyond the compre-
hension of my limited faculties? But the conception
of the God-man is divine, and I feel its self-evidencing
power in its suitability to all my spiritual wants. When
I take hold of the person of Christ with a simple, but
firm faith, I find in Him the key to all mysteries. God
out of Christ is doubtless abundantly evidenced in the
worlds He has created; but he is an abstraction,—
a Being at an infinite distance from the human soul.
In the God-man He is brought near, heaven is ever
open to us, and all heavenly blessings descend upon
our waiting souls."

In those days of compulsory leisure he kept up an
extensive correspondence, and several of his letters at
this time are in a similar tone to the above. He had,
a short time before, been reading Dorner's great
work on the development of the doctrine concerning
the person of Christ; and the variations of opinion on
the subject in the history of the Church had evidently
led him to think and speak often of the necessity of
distinguishing between a practical living faith on the
Saviour and a speculative theory, which might be a
dead theory after all, about the nature of His person.

or work. He is also naturally led, in devout prostration of the spirit before the divine person and work, to question with himself, whether the busy occupation of his life with external affairs had not unduly withdrawn his attention from spiritual realities; and he therefore finds a certain consolation in the enforced retirement, which gave him larger opportunities than he had for a long time enjoyed of earnest communion with his own spirit and with the Eternal Father of spirits. It was not only natural, it was commendable, that he should enter into such earnest self-questioning. But, happily, he never fell into any morbid religious sentiment, which would have made him regret that he had spent his energies rather in the service of others than in any selfish concern for the supposed salvation of his own soul. He knew that the only salvation the soul needs is salvation from the curse of selfishness, and that that salvation is found in a life which follows the footsteps of the Lord Jesus Christ by devout self-sacrifice to intelligent labour for the good of mankind. Even the need of the spirit for religious meditation and the indulgence of religious emotion was not allowed by him to induce a neglect of the more imperious obligations of practical beneficence. But the record of his religious life in a previous chapter shows that even the absorb-

ing cares of his numerous occupations had never led
him to undervalue the means of religious culture.   He
had long accustomed himself to solemn reflection on
eternal things, and even to that "meditation of death,"
in which it has been said that all true wisdom consists.
As a specimen of such solitary musings may be quoted
a record, dated 12th August, 1876, jotted down in one
of his note-books :—

"This week has been St. James' Day Fair with the
usual races.   Owing to the cessation of business, I
have enjoyed with much zest two days of tranquillity
and pleasant domestic retirement.   Yesterday, in company with my wife and four of our grandchildren, I
visited our beautiful cemetery.   At all times I love
such a visit, and never fail to find it profitable.   There
lies the dust of my two daughters ; and now when the
poignancy of grief is subdued by time, there is a soothing influence in recalling the memories of the dear
departed on the spot where their ashes rest.   There,
too, in close proximity, are deposited three infant
grandchildren, whose brief span of existence in this
mysterious life did not enable them to see or feel much
of its joys and sorrows.

"On occasion of this visit there were circumstances
which involuntarily led me into a new series of reflec-

tions. From the high ground of the cemetery I could see the dark moving mass congregated on the race-course, eagerly seeking pleasure in what, to say the least, is not a very elevating pursuit. I could not help feeling the contrast between the noisy bustle of the race-ground and the stillness of 'God's Acre.' Yonder were forty thousand human beings, all unmindful of the twenty thousand who were sleeping here, unconscious of the noise and excitement so near to them. How solemn the thought that in a few short years that moving mass of men, now so intent on pleasure, would be all occupants of some city of the dead! 'Vanity of vanities; all is vanity!'

" I cannot say that I yet feel any very marked bodily symptoms of old age, although I am now nearing the seventy years which are the allotted span of human life. But I confess I had a strange feeling to-day, when walking among the tombs—a feeling as if I were more at home among them than in the busiest part of the town. There is not a name on any of those numerous monuments which I did not recognize as that of some former acquaintance,—scarcely a grave whose occupant I was not wont to meet in the intercourse of daily life. I feel, therefore, as if there I were among my old friends and acquaintances, while in the town there is a generation rising up who are to me strangers. Something akin to this feeling I find on opening my morning newspaper. I quite unconsciously turn to the obituary notices, even before the political and other news : the births and marriages do not interest me at all.

"In the midst of such reflections as these, reminding me, if not by bodily weakness, by reasons and feelings quite as unmistakable, that my lease of life is nearly expired, I cannot feel too grateful to the bountiful Giver of all our blessings, that I am still privileged to retain all the freshness of feeling which I had in my youth. My dear partner, who has now for more than forty years shared all the alternate joys and sorrows of our married life, has grown old with me ; but our feelings of mutual affection are as fresh as in the days of 'love's young dream.' O that I could lay these lessons to heart, and be preparing to meet the great and solemn change that must now at no distant date come to me ! God grant that I may be given such dispositions and affections here, as will fit me for the enjoyment of that blessedness hereafter, which is prepared for those who love and do the truth."

To a spirit accustomed to such "meditations on the tombs" the prospect of death came with no surprise.

As soon as the fatal issue appeared probable, even possible, he spoke and wrote of it, not often, only when it was naturally suggested, and never with a mere bravado. His words are always but the natural expression of a contented resignation to the Divine Will growing out of the conviction that that Will rules all things, and rules all things well.

About the middle of July he enjoyed a respite from suffering for a few days; but though the interval revived the hopes of his friends, he himself made use of it to set his house in order. It was during this period, on Sunday the 13th, that he conducted worship with his family for the last time. He had a larger number with him than usual on that day, and he seemed to find a more than usual satisfaction in having the opportunity of leading them once more to the Pitiful Father of us all. He was too weak to rise from bed, and he had to ask one of his children to read the lesson which he selected from the fifteenth chapter of the first epistle to the Corinthians; but supported on his pillow, he led their devotions in a prayer which is memorable to them all for its peculiarly exalted tone.

At the end of that week, on the 19th of July, a relapse occurred, from which he never rallied. At times

K

his suffering was intense. Once, when in great distress, he said to his daughter, " I'm wearying to get away home. Ask Almighty God that it may not be long." On two consecutive days he asked her to read to him the thirteenth and fourteenth chapters of St. John's Gospel, and a favourite hymn of Montgomery's beginning,

> " Friend after friend departs ;
>   Who hath not lost a friend ?
> There is no union here of hearts,
>   That finds not here an end :
> Were this frail world our only rest,
> Living or dying, none were blest."

On Sunday morning, the 27th of July, he asked for Toplady's "Rock of Ages,"—a hymn in which he took a particular delight. His family gathered round his bed, and sang it to him, while he seemed still vigorous enough to follow it throughout, and to derive comfort from the words and tones. After this, however, he became too feeble for continuous attention, and it was only at intervals that he appeared to take notice of what was going on around him.

Meanwhile, in answer to a cable message, I had left Quebec on the 19th of July. Favoured by the weather all the way, our ship cast anchor in the Mersey before dawn on the 28th, so that I was able to reach Paisley on the afternoon of that day. He had not been informed that I was telegraphed for, and it required a few minutes to break the news after I entered his room. As soon as he comprehended that I was there, he clasped his hands over his breast as if—one might be allowed to imagine—he were repeating in silent gratitude, "Now lettest Thou Thy servant depart in peace." Two or three times during the evening and night he asked for me again, showing that, at intervals when consciousness rallied, he was aware of my having come. On the following morning he passed quietly away.

Of the funeral I should have said nothing, but for an incident which was more touching than all the expressions of respect implied in the pomp and show of the occasion. On the evening before the funeral, a number of working men, knowing that many of their class would be prevented from taking part in the ceremony owing to their want of the dress considered appropriate to such occasions, appointed a representative to inquire whether they would be allowed to join the procession in their work-day clothes. On learning that this would be regarded by the family as a manifestation of good feeling, and that the public authorities, who had charge of the funeral, would make no objection, a bill was posted over the town in the morning, inviting working men to fall into line with the procession as they came from their work in the afternoon, and, considering the shortness of the notice, a large number acted upon the invitation. Many may object to the pomp of a public funeral as incongruous with an occasion so eloquent with its lesson of the littleness of man, and to many all the trappings of our funeral show may be distasteful, expressive as they are only of an unchristian gloom unrelieved by one cheerful symbol of an immortal life. But an unceremonious outburst of feeling, like that of these working men, is one, the genuineness of which it is impossible to mistake.

www.ingramcontent.com/pod-product-compliance
Lightning Source LLC
Chambersburg PA
CBHW020234030726
47497CB00009B/3084